When Rafe got off the
cars parked in front of the s
the wide steps leading up t
Mr. Bowding, was deep in discussion with
officer prowled around the side of the school, in front of a section of the beige brick that was marked with a green smear of graffiti. Rafe momentarily forgot about his problems with Toby and headed toward the graffiti.

"It's just nonsense," one of the seniors said. His cheeks and chin were covered with little blood-spotted tissues, as if he'd had a disaster shaving that morning.

"Looks like paisley," his friend replied—this kid had a significant overbite.

Idiots, thought Rafe. He had seen thousands of these tags in his neighborhood. After a while, you could read them. They were the street version of runes or Tolkien's Elvish script. This tag was a metallic green, the color of a dragon's scale.

Tissue-Face said, "You'd think that if you were going to vandalize something, you'd at least have something to say."

Over-Bite replied, "You know *they* can't read, much less spell."

Before he thought better of it, Rafe said, "It says 'Mantis.' There are probably others just like that one."

Both seniors turned and looked at him, as if he'd suddenly materialized out of thin air. They wore twin expressions of incredulity, mouths hanging open like doofuses. It was beautiful. But short-lived.

The police officers and the vice principal broke up the gathering of gawking students and ushered them into the school. All the chatter as he went down the hall was about the graffiti. Rafe heard boys excitedly talking about drug-turf wars, like you saw on *Law & Order* or *The Wire*. Rafe didn't see what the big deal was, or even why the cops were called in the first place. At Garvey, markings like these were common. The side of the school was a palimpsest of tags, drawings, and long-abandoned murals. You just got the janitor to cover up the worst ones with that awful rust-red paint. But that was the difference between Garvey and Our Shady Lady. Red paint would never suffice for the pristine walls of the school. They'd probably have to be repainted. Rafe had a quick, evil thought: he hoped that Mantis would show up again, should the walls be repainted.

Also by Craig Laurance Gidney:

Sea, Swallow Me and Other Stories

Bereft

Craig Laurance Gidney

Tiny Satchel Press
Philadelphia

A portion of *Bereft* first appeared in different form in *From Where We Sit: Black Writers Write Black Youth*, edited by Victoria A. Brownworth, Tiny Satchel Press, 2011.

Tiny Satchel Press
311 West Seymour Street
Philadelphia, PA 19144
tinysatchelpress@gmail.com
www.tinysatchelpress.com

Distributed by
Bella Books P.O. Box
10543 Tallahassee, FL
32302 1-800-729-4992

Publisher/Art director: Maddy Gold
Editor-in-Chief: Victoria A. Brownworth
Cover design: Christopher Bauer
Cover production: Jennifer Mercer
Book design: Caroline Curtis
Tiny Satchel Press logo: Chris Angelucci

Printed in the United States of America.
First edition. ISBN 978-0-9849146-4-7

To O, who helped me survive childhood.

My mother bore me in the southern wild,
And I am black, but O! my soul is white;
White as an angel is the English child,
But I am black, as if bereav'd of light.

—William Blake, "The Little Black Boy"

Building the Mask

This is how you make a mask:

It starts with the materials. Wood from a sacred tree, the one hidden deep in the forest, covered in lichen and moss and dripping with vines. Shells found on the beach—cowries that look like mouths about to speak, shells white as chips of bone. Thin stalks of grass, baked by the sun to a yellow-brown color, tough as whips. Paint made from the pulp of flowers bright as blood and leaves that shimmer with indigo and cerise. The tusks and teeth of vicious, totemic animals. The intricate feathers of birds that soar and hunt above the wilderness. Each of these things must be chosen carefully: the right piece of wood, paint the right shade. When the right pieces are chosen, the mask lives, fed by their energies. The mask will be more than a decoration.

Carving isn't about finding the right angle and plane of the wood. It's about finding the face that's already there, hidden in the whorls and the grain. Tools are needed to reveal the face, but the real skill is the vision that unearths the eyes and the mouth and the other features.

Once the shape is clear, fine details can be filled in. The skin of this mask, for instance, will be black, the black made of all colors, so that in certain light, there will be a note of green, a whisper of purple, a hint of brown. Shells surround the face, feathers curl from its ears.

The best masks do more than hide the wearers' faces. They reveal what is hidden in their souls.

CHAPTER ONE
OUR LADY

"Why is it called Our Lady of the Woods?" Rafe asked. "There are no woods around."

"I don't know—it's a Catholic thing," his mother answered. She stepped out of the bus cautiously, as if she was afraid the sidewalk would swallow her up. She put her hand on Rafe's shoulder to steady herself. Rafe walked slowly, mindful of this. Mom was doing better than she had the last couple of days.

The school was just a block away from the bus stop. Rafe felt—he was unsure of what he felt. *Excitement? Dread?* When they stood at the bottom of the stairs leading up to the entrance, he could label the feeling immediately: *intimidation.* He glanced at his mother. She was silent, too. Could she be feeling the same thing?

The school looked like a church. Within a stone mouth, a pair of wooden doors stood guard, looking at the two of them with windows like honeycombed glass eyes. If the sidewalk didn't swallow them, then maybe the school would.

"It looks like that school that Harry Potter goes to," Rafe's Mom said. She adjusted her purse strap—something she always did when she was nervous. "What's it called?"

"Hogwarts," Rafe said. But he thought it didn't look

like Hogwarts at all. It was too *clean*. Magic didn't live here.

"Come on," said his mother, and they began to climb the stairs.

Behind the doors, it looked like any other school, with linoleum tiles and dull fluorescent lights. A sign pointed toward the administration offices. There was a carpeted waiting room, where his mother told him to sit while she approached a desk and spoke with the white-haired lady sitting behind a computer screen. The magazines on the small coffee table were terrible. They were a mixture of religious tracts and issues of something called *Catholic Youth*, years out of date. The kids on the cover looked way too happy. Rafe wished he had his Nintendo DS or even a book. He didn't have to wait too long, though. His mother returned and sat next to him.

"Look at me," she commanded him. She inspected his face for any invisible grime. Finding none, she said, "Sit up straight." And he did.

She was about to give him some further instruction, but was interrupted when a boy lightly tapped on his mother's shoulder and said, "Hello, I'm Angus O'Connell, the school chaplain."

Rafe realized the young man wasn't an older teenager—he just looked like one. He was taller than both Rafe and his mother, with hair as dark as the vestments he wore. His eyes were the color of root beer.

Rafe's mother stood and shook his hand. "I'm Ursele, and this here is my son, Rafael Fannen."

Angus shook Rafe's hand vigorously, over-eagerly, Rafe thought. Rafe mumbled, "Nice to meet you, Mr. O'Connell."

"Please," he said, "Everyone calls me Angus. If it's okay, I'd like to give you both a tour of the school. We're all so happy to have Rafael as a Toussaint Scholar!"

He led them out into the hall, walking briskly as he chatted away. Rafe took his mother's hand and she leaned into him. O'Connell—for some reason, Rafe didn't want to call him Angus, he wasn't going to be fake-friends with anybody—was a good six feet ahead of them.

"Yo, hold up," Rafe said.

O'Connell stopped in mid-stride. It was an absurd pose—almost as if he were playing a game of Stop Light. He pivoted like a dancer, faced them.

"I'm sorry. It's these gosh-darn legs of mine—Oh!" He scuttled back to them. "Are you okay, Ms. Fannen?"

"Quite. It's just that my sciatica is acting up. You two go on ahead. I'll catch up."

"No, no. I can go slower. It's just that sometimes this old noggin of mine isn't as observant as it could be." O'Connell tapped the side of his head, like Rafe had seen his grandmother do with under-ripe melons.

Rafe thought, *This dude is a serious goof. 'Gosh-darn?' What's next, 'gee whiz?' Will everyone be like him?*

The three of them eventually made it to a classroom. What was behind the door made Rafe smile, in spite of himself. Each desk—every single one—had a computer. And, unlike the computer lab at Garvey, each computer was new. The front of the classroom had a standard black board, but there was an LCD projector chained to a cart that pointed to the front. Even Rafe's mother said, "Oh my," under her breath. As O'Connell went over each feature of the classroom, Rafe longed to touch just one pristine keyboard, fire up one screen.

"Do you know how to type?" O'Connell asked him.

"A little. I hunt and peck."

"We have a software program that can teach you how to touch type."

Rafe's mother said, "Oh," and fidgeted with her purse.

O'Connell looked at her, encouraging her to explain.

"It's just, well. The laptop we have—had—it's broken. And it'll be a while before I can afford one." She looked embarrassed.

"Hmmm," O'Connell said. Rafe could see the phantom light bulb flicker above his head. "That shouldn't be a problem. I'll have to check with the IT department, but I'm sure an arrangement can be made to rent one of the older laptops while you're waiting. In fact, I'll make it a priority."

Rafe's mother visibly relaxed.

The tour continued. There was the music room, which was arranged like an amphitheater, a forest of music stands by the black baby-grand piano. The auditorium had a stage hidden by a deep red curtain. They stepped outside, onto the playing fields. Beyond the blacktop, which was fringed with a running track, there was a sea of yellow, early fall grass, hemmed in by soccer nets. The tour ended with a visit to the chapel.

O'Connell quipped, "Here's my lair, if you will."

It was a miniature church, shrunk to the size of one room. It smelled like a church, spicy and musky, with an overtone of candle wax. The floor was gray slate that held the cold. Two aisles of pews faced a dais that was covered in velvet carpet the color of poinsettias at their peak. There was an altar emblazoned with an intricate cross. Framed behind it all, a woman made of porcelain seemed to float against a black velvet backdrop. Her arms were spread out in a gesture of welcoming embrace. Two containers filled with lilies that had seen better days were placed at her bare feet.

"How lovely," said Rafe's mother in her best White Lady-ese.

O'Connell looked almost looked bashful. "I try, Ma'am."

In spite of himself, Rafe had to agree. It *was* beautiful. He approached the stone virgin. *How did they get the stone so white? Why did she seem to glow?* There was a half-smile on her face. She reminded him of Galadriel, the elf queen from *The Lord of the Rings.* All she needed was a mirror pool. But as Rafe examined her closely, he felt that there was something creepy about her. He couldn't quite put his finger on it.

Rafe's mother was speaking to O'Connell: "We used to go to Imani Faith Temple, on Rose Street."

"I know the one. I've been to a service there. Quite beautiful."

"Yes. We make it there every once in a while."

"Well, if it's okay with you, Mrs. Fannen, I would like a have a quick chat with Rafael."

Rafe turned from the floating Virgin—and knew immediately what was so weird about her. She had no eyes. Just white spaces—almond-shaped depressions where irises should have been. Like a mannequin that could suddenly come to life.

O'Connell asked Rafe's mother to stay in the small chapel. She looked grateful to finally sit down. He led

Rafe to a small office just to the side of the chapel. There was a pristine MacBook on a desk cluttered with prayer books and hymnals.

"I thought we'd rap for just a bit," O'Connell said. He used finger-quotes around the word "rap." Rafe hated that gesture.

Rafe nodded at him.

"First, do you have any questions? Concerns? Are you excited? Scared? It's okay, you can tell me. Everything we say is between you and me."

Rafe had nothing to say, but it was getting uncomfortable. O'Connell's eyes were intense. "I'm good," Rafe said.

"Well, we're good too! I mean, Our Lady of the Woods is pleased to have you. You know, you tested very high. I'm not supposed to say so, but I don't think it's bad to let you know that you are one of our most promising students, at least on paper."

"Um. Cool..."

"We're committed to diversifying the student population. In a way, you're a pioneer."

"Cool." Rafe was less sure as he said it this time.

"You know that you can come to me."

"Yes..."

There was something O'Connell was holding back, it seemed. He was nervous. "I really want you to succeed here," he began. "Rafael," O'Connell continued—he wasn't looking at Rafe directly—"Our Lady of the Woods, as you know, has a dress code."

What was he on about? Of course, Rafe knew about the dress code—the burgundy blazer with some sort of shield on the pocket, grey slacks, white dress shirt. Was the chaplain angry that he wasn't wearing it *now*? School didn't start for another two weeks.

"Was I supposed to wear the uniform today, Mr. O'Connell?"

"Oh, no!" O'Connell laughed nervously. "That's not what I meant at all. What I'm trying to say is this. The dress code here is a bit—*draconian*. It extends to things like... facial hair. And haircuts." The chaplain winced at that last word.

His hair. Rafe felt it against his neck, each locked tendril, roots that varied in shade from black to auburn. It had taken him almost two years to get it this length. He'd fought with his mother for the right to have his hair look this way.

"You mean I have to cut it off?" That came out a little more harshly than he wanted it to.

The chaplain sighed. "I'm afraid so. They—the school has very strict guidelines about this. It's in the handbook, even. If it were up to me... But it's not. I hate being the bearer of bad news."

Rafe wanted to curse. His hair was the one thing he really liked about himself. His voice was squeaky and sounded like a little boy's at times. He seemed to have stopped growing—neither his mother nor his father were particularly tall. Acne would erupt and wage volcanic war on his face every now and then. Rafe knew, when he'd been accepted, that he would have to make some concessions—the hour-long bus ride across town, the stiff, dorky clothing. But not his damned hair!

The two of them sat in silence for a moment more.

Rafe broke the silence. "Okay."

O'Connell got up from behind his desk. "Good

man!" He held out his hand. Rafe offered his, reluctantly. The vicar clasped it tightly. He was so tall that Rafe could look right up into his nostrils. He saw darkness in those pin-prick holes. Darkness and hair. Rafe almost laughed. Almost.

"Let's go back to your mother, young man." Rafe stood, and headed to the office door. But as he left, he felt the most feather-soft touch on the back of his head. He half turned, then stopped. It was as if—but it couldn't be—as if O'Connell had touched his hair, lightly, briefly. But he wouldn't do that, would he? Rafe knew about the scandals between Catholic clergy and choir boys. But he didn't count. Choirboys were blond children with ice-blue eyes and cherubic, pink cheeks.

Rafe's mother was checking the voicemail on her cellphone in the back pew of the chapel. Mr. O'Connell walked them to the front door. He and Rafe's mom chatted about the arrangements for a laptop.

Rafe helped his mother down the stairs. At the bottom of the stairs, she asked how he liked the school. They were at the bus stop before he answered.

"I don't like it."

She fidgeted with her purse. "Why not?"

"I just *don't*."

She didn't say anything more until they were on the 43 cross-town bus. The bus passed by gingerbread houses on landscaped hills, two-story homes with large front lawns, and high-rise condominiums guarded by stone lions, then it crossed the dividing street, leading to the more familiar terrain of liquor stores, *bodegas*, and Section 8 housing. The bus slowly filled up with construction workers and young mothers with squirming children.

"What did you and that guy—Angus—talk about?" she asked.

Is Mom psychic? Rafe wondered. She got right to the heart of the matter.

Rafe sighed. "He wants me to cut my hair. Says it's against the dress code."

She made a tsking sound with her teeth. "That's it? That's why you don't like the school? I don't like that policy, either. I mean, they're dreadlocks, not you wearing them droopy saggy pants kids seem to like these days. But, Rafael, you can't screw up this opportunity. Is your hairstyle worth a full scholarship?"

He looked at the grooved floor of the bus. "No," he said quietly.

He didn't have to look up to know that she was probably nodding. "Keep your eyes on the prize, honey," she said.

They got off the bus ten minutes later, right in front of their apartment building. A group of girls were jumping Double Dutch, the ropes slicing the air with a rhythmic sound. Some teenage boys sat on a bench, sharing earphones, mouthing along to some lyrics. Rafe caught the words *nigga* and *ho* in the litany. Pigeons pecked at the neon-bright crumbs of cheese curls and corn chips.

The elevator stank of booze and old weed. In fact, there was a quarter-full 40 leaning against the back of the elevator. Rafe noticed fresh graffiti on the scratched elevator doors. *PUTA,* it proclaimed blackly in wet permanent marker.

Rafe's mother suddenly said, "That kid, Angus, wouldn't last a minute here."

Rafe smiled. “He’s like Opie, or something.”

“Now, now. He’s nice enough. I mean that. But he’s what your father and I used to call ‘Hardcore White.’ You know, he reminds me of that jerky boss on that show, *The Office*. Good heart, but clueless.”

Rafe laughed. “He told me that that he wanted to *rap* with me.”

“Lord. You *know* his momma calls us *colored*.”

Rafe woke up around 2 am. A car chugged down the street, spouting a Jay-Z song ten times too loud, followed by the arthritic rumble of a bus. He remembered a dream—the skeins of it faded by degrees. Images floated around his head. Boys in crisp uniforms with glowing blue eyes. Burning roses. Crushed velvet, red as blood. The anemic cleanliness of an Apple store. White candles, gray smoke. And through it all, the eyeless face of Galadriel. She held out her hands to him.

Our Lady of the Woods hovered above it all—the school, the block, his life.

There were no woods near him, of course. She was Our Lady of Concrete.

CHAPTER TWO
Dreads

White Elephant Mall was about a two-hour bus ride, even though it was only fifteen minutes outside of the city. It was just that the bus went on such a meandering route, through strip malls, residential neighborhoods, and even, at one point, what looked like farmland. When he was visiting his father, Rafe made sure that he had plenty of distractions to keep the trip from being too boring. He'd stopped reading *Lord of the Flies*, which had been on Our Lady of the Woods' summer reading list, because his stop was approaching and he didn't want to miss it. Old-school rap pounded from his earbuds—a mix that this father had made, groups like KRS-One and Public Enemy, music that had a "message," not that "woman-hating stuff" Rafe usually listened to, his father said. Not that Rafe really paid much attention to the words anyway—it was the whoosh, wow, and flutter of sounds and samples that entranced him.

The stop was a block away from White Elephant Mall. A sudden heat wave was in effect. Rafe walked on the radiant sidewalks to the dead shopping center. White Marsh Mall rose from a sea of empty blacktop parking spaces like a square volcano. White Marsh Mall used to be a destination mall back in the 90s, before some vague financial disaster caused all of the major chains and restaurants that used to bolster it to close. It was called White Elephant Mall because of the caravan of unwanted shops and restaurants that appeared—and, just as quickly, vanished—from the landscape.

"It's where all old stores go to die," one of his friends back at Garvey once said. And it was true. He went through the empty corridor. A major department store was closed; a wasteland of nude mannequins stared out from behind the bars of a grate. Olde Time Buffet added the odor of heat-lamped food to the air. One open store sold seascapes in lurid colors and pictures of creepy clowns. Another sold electric fiber-art sculptures that looked like Dr. Seuss creatures. Rafe's father's kiosk was in between a nail shop and a discount shoe store.

The kiosk had three sections. One was a cart full of African sculptures of elephants, gazelles, and zebras, carved in dark wood. Another cart held black soap, shea butter, and incense. Between the two carts was a garden of masks, in various shapes and sizes. Stylized eyes and lips leered at Rafe. Rafe's father sat in front of one of them, a wooden face with a fringe of straw like a ruff.

"Pops," Rafe said, as he took out his earbuds. His father turned to him, then stood and awkwardly hugged him.

"Help me," said his father, and Rafe joined him in constructing the audience of masks. Rafe had a feeling that this latest venture of his father's was doomed to failure. Hardly anyone came to the mall, let alone to this kiosk, and the price of the masks was not insignificant. But at the same time, Rafe was proud that his father was doing this work—it was less shady than the other schemes he'd had in the past. When the kiosk, called "Chiwara: African Art" was set up, Rafe's father left to go to the bathroom. For some reason, he carried a gym bag with him. Rafe sat on the stool in front of the kiosk. He knew it was unlikely that anyone would buy anything. The discount shoe store was the busiest store in the entire mall. Asian ladies in surgical masks gazed listlessly at the aimlessly milling mothers and kids from the nail shop's storefront. Rafe could barely stand the chemical tang that drifted from it. A radio station piped in bland music from hidden speakers in the mall. Rafe contemplated an antelope sculpture with wooden horns that rose up like those famous M. C. Escher stairs.

Behind a jungle of plastic plants there was another kiosk. This one sold cell-phone covers in all shapes, colors, and fabrics. Bejeweled, silicone, and aluminum cases hung on locked hooks. Rafe watched an Asian man, no taller than he was, begin to set up his kiosk. The man was rail-thin; it looked like you could easily break his bones. His hair was black, crested by a wave of white-blond. Maybe five earrings dangled from each earlobe. His music was up way too loud—Rafe could hear the unmistakable chords of a Lady Gaga song.

Rafe looked away from him, disgusted. Why did he have to be so... *gay?*

Pops came back at that moment. He was dressed in a new shirt. His gray dreads were neatly tied up with a leather string. His skin looked radiant and soft. Had he shaved in the mall bathroom? It certainly looked like he had. But why would he do that *here?*

Surely, he could have done that at home? Rafe had never been to his father's home—there was always an excuse or story. Rafe found that he didn't really want to think about it.

"Any customers?" Pops asked, deadpan.

"Tons," Rafe replied.

Rafe's father started the endless hours of re-arranging merchandise, as if each minuscule move would somehow summon a horde of shoppers. Rafe reached into his book bag and fished out *Lord of the Flies*. He really wanted to play with his Nintendo DS, but he knew that his father would ask him about homework. His parents didn't like each other, but they both were in agreement about his study habits.

"How'd you like the school?" his father asked.

"It looks like a horror movie set," Rafe said, and Pops laughed. "I mean, it's got all these echoing halls, and creepy-ass saints staring at you. I know when the lights go out, they all come to life. You just know it."

"Well, make the best of it. Just view it as a stepping stone."

"I know, Pops."

A potential customer—a woman with a magenta top with a kid in tow—stopped by the kiosk. While she inspected the wares, Rafe moved away as his Dad tried on his sales persona. He sounded knowledgeable about the pieces—talking about the countries and villages where they were crafted, the religious significance of the masks. The mask faces seemed to follow Rafe's movements. Somehow, the wood and straw and shells, the patterns, the geometric shapes, were more comforting to Rafe than that stone lady's eyeless gaze. The masks had no eyes, either, but they invited you to place your own face against the grain and stare outward. The stone lady was anything but inviting. She was cold and wanted to be worshipped.

"Hey, you Sam's kid?"

Rafe had wandered to the other side of the plastic jungle, next to the cell-phone cover kiosk, "Bling My Ring." The blond Asian guy sat on what looked like a director's chair.

"Yeah." "Cool. I'm Quy, but everyone calls me Q."

Q waited for Rafe to respond. He supposed he had to. The crystal skull earrings Q wore were distracting. "I'm Rafe."

"Ray?"

"No, Rafe—short for Rafael."

"Oh, yes. Ha ha. Like the Ninja Turtle."

Rafe must have scowled. O'Connell would have said something that dorky. Q said, "Sorry. You must get that all the time."

I did. When I was five. "Naw, that's cool." He took Q's offered hand. It was really no bigger than his own.

"Your dad's great. He told me all about those masks. I call him the Professor. Ha ha."

Rafe nodded. He tried not to look directly at Q. Q's flamboyancy was too much. The way he talked, the way his hands moved like little hummingbirds, the way he spazzed out to his iPod was too... *faggy*. Maybe he wasn't actually a fag, but still. His voice and personality were as gaudy as the cell-phone covers he sold. All *Hello Kitty* and encrusted with pink and aqua rhinestones.

Rafe saw that the customer had left. He nodded at Q and went back to his father.

"I see you met my buddy, Q-tip," Pops said.

"Uh huh." Rafe was kind of disappointed that Q was a "buddy" of his father's. Pops wasn't a thug, not by a long shot. But he'd had his problems, including a six-month lock-up for missing child support payments a couple of years ago. Rafe remembered visiting him a couple of times at the minimum-security prison. The bright orange jumpsuits, the endless gray fields, the yellow cinderblock—the colors of desolation. Some of the men looked rough, their faces hard and carved with hatred and ink-pen tattoos. Somehow, his father had survived that, and managed to scrape together one kind of living or another. Rafe never asked what it was like behind the bars. He didn't really want to know. But he imagined that Pops had seen his fair share of terrible things. Things were better now.

"Pops," he said, "there's this thing about the school." *There were several things about the school, but there was no need for Rafe to overburden him.* "They have a dress code."

"Yeah? I assumed that it would. You need money for uniforms or something? Listen, tell your ma that business has been kind of slow—you know, the economy and everything—"

"No—that's not it. I mean, we could always use the money. But this dress code—this priest dude told me that the dress code even included hairstyles."

Rafe let that sink in for a moment.

His father sputtered, "Hairstyles? Like moustaches and—no. *No*. They don't mean—not your dreads."

"Yeah. The priest dude, he asked me to cut my dreads. He said that it violated the standards of student appearance. He gave me the student handbook. Just a moment..."

Rafe opened his book bag and went through it until he found the handbook. It was in the school colorsburgundy with pewter lettering. The picture on the front showed a group of well-groomed boys, mostly white, sitting around a goofily grinning Angus O'Connell on the steps of the school.

"That's him—the priest dude. His name is Angus. Like a hamburger." Rafe flipped to the page where it listed student grooming. *"Young men must have sensible haircuts. Hair dyes or extravagant styles are not permitted. Hair must be above the collar."* He handed his father the book, and watched him read the sentence and suck his teeth in frustration.

"Man, they can't..." his father started. "What does your ma say?"

"That I should cut my hair."

Rafe's father sighed. His own gray dreads flowed down his back like a river of roots. His mom and dad had never been together, not while Rafe was alive. Though they didn't say it, Rafe had the feeling that he was the result of a booty call. He knew that his mother would never have aborted him, nor given him up for adoption. Religion simmered beneath the surface with her, even if it never came to a boil. His father was not religious at all. Before prison, he was openly contemptuous of Rafe's mother's occasional forays to Imani Faith Temple. He thought that Catholicism was mind-poison. After prison, Rafe's father began to investigate more African-based spirituality, in a sort of academic manner, so he became more tolerant of Rafe's mother's bouts of church-going. Well, barely tolerant. Rafe couldn't imagine why they ever got together in the first place. His dad thought his mom was a fool. His mom thought his dad was a bad man—bad enough to send him to jail. They hated each other—maybe not with a hot, *Wrath of Khan* type of anger. No. It was a *mature,* grown-up hatred. Rafe thought of Jadis, the White Witch from *The Lion, The Witch and the Wardrobe.* Theirs was a cold, considered hatred.

So it was kind of shocking to hear what his father said next. "I agree with her."

Rafe saw that it took every ounce of his father's willpower to utter those words. It was like he was fighting against some evil mindforce.

"I don't like it. How could I? The African body is sacred. Dreadlocks are sacred—just like these masks. But there's something more important at stake here. Your ma and I never finished high school. We had you instead. This scholarship is—"

"An opportunity," Rafe finished for him. "Don't you think I know that? Damn, I'm beginning to hate that word. I *will* get the damn haircut—but I don't have to like it, do I?"

His dad smiled and patted him on his back. "You certainly don't. I know it's hard."

Rafe shrugged him off. "I'll be back. I'm just gonna take a walk."

Rafe left his father and White Elephant Mall. Outside, he could clear his head. The sea of blacktop shimmered in the heat. A jitney from a nearby old folks home rolled up and a group of seniors stepped out, with their walkers and canes. Another bus zoomed down the highway, spitting out exhaust and a veil of smoke. Rafe began to sweat and considered going back inside when he saw, a couple of rows away, his father's van. For no particular reason, he went toward it.

It used to be sleek and black, like a panther made of metal. Now the black was obscured by film, and in spots, faded by the sun. Bird droppings spattered the outside of the van, as if it had sat there for a while. That was odd. His father used to take care of the van as if it were a child. Rafe's mother once remarked that the van had been his new wife. Rafe remembered looking into the cool black mirror and seeing his reflection. He glanced inside the tinted glass of the driver's-side front window. Merchandise spilled over everything—wooden zebras, lions, and antelopes seemed to cover every surface, as if the van were Noah's Ark. There was litter, too—old Chinese-takeout boxes, half-empty sodas. It looked like it stank in there. And with the temperature outside, it probably did. Then Rafe saw, toward the back of the van, what looked like a bed. Hillocks of pillows peeked out from a rumpled comforter.

Rafe had no words for what he was feeling. His father must live here. That was why Rafe had never been to his father's new apartment—*this* was the apartment. After examining it for what seemed like forever, Rafe moved away from the van.

He walked across the tarmac, which had softened from the heat and held the impression of his sneakers like black snow. *Should I ask him about it?* Immediately, the word *No!* floated in front of him, like a comic-book thought-balloon. And he wouldn't talk to his mom about it—definitely. She didn't need that extra stress.

Inside the cool air of the White Elephant, he slowly walked back to the Chiwara kiosk. He felt guilty—he knew a secret that his father didn't want him to know about. Rafe had just gotten over the idea that parents weren't psychic—he now knew that their ability to sense when you'd done something wrong had more to do with a kid's body language and facial expressions. Rafe was half-tempted to go to the restroom and practice a poker face. He deep-sixed that idea and went to the food court instead.

The pickings were pitiful. In the event of a zombie apocalypse, White Elephant Mall would be a poor place to hole up in. A bored Latino teenager manned a Smootheez store. An Asian grandma read the paper at Jade Dragon. Luigi's pizza looked heat-lamped to death—triangular globs of yellow grease. Rafe settled on some crinkle fries and an energy drink from the burger place. He ate in the neon-lit gloom; he was the only person in the seating area. When he got back to his dad's kiosk, he could always claim indigestion—the fries were heavy with oil.

His father was chatting with Q when Rafe returned. They were laughing at something. Q's hands flew around like nervous butterflies. *Why can't he tone it down?* In the hood, Q would be beaten to a pulp, or he might be lucky and only be called *faggot*. Q was so thin, he'd be snapped like a twig.

For no particular reason—or maybe spite, if he were honest—Rafe brashly interrupted them.

"Dad, can I talk to you? Alone?"

"Talk to you later, Sam," Q said, backing away. He

gave one of his bright—*too bright*—smiles to Rafe and went to the other side of the plastic jungle divider.

When they were as alone as they could be, his dad asked, "What's this about?"

And there was a moment. Time stopped, and Rafe said, *I know your secret. Why are you sleeping in your car? Is there anything I can do? Anyway I can help? Maybe Mom and I could have you live with us, only for a little while, so you could get back on your feet.* But what came out was, "I want you to take me to the barber's. Today."

Rafe's father grinned at him, clapped him on the shoulder. "There's a place in the mall. We'll go there after I close up shop."

Rafe nodded. He tried to make his face as stoic as possible. His heart felt heavy. He carried his father's secret like it was the One Ring and he was Frodo. He knew that this would be a secret he would keep inside. It would lay quietly next to his other shames—the other unuttered, unthinkable things.

The rest of the day went by slowly. Rafe finished *Lord of the Flies* and started on his other summer history of the early church, which was as boring as the empty mall. He ended up breaking out his Nintendo and playing a game. There were maybe three customers that day, and they all bought black soap and shea butter. Rafe's dad did some half-assed pitching of artwork, to no avail. One lady remarked that one of the masks looked devilish and she couldn't bear to have something evil looking at her while she slept. What could you say to that?

Around 4:30, they began to close down. Since business was slow (was it ever brisk?), they would take an extended break and go to the barber's. The masks were removed from their stands and locked in the kiosk carts.

"Hey, Pops," said Rafe, holding a mask that intrigued him. The face had round eyeholes and thick lips. A halo of polished cowrie shells surrounded the face, which had been carved of wood that was almost Rafe's same skin tone. He put his eyes up to the holes and peered out. The world didn't look any different, but Rafe felt something just the same. Maybe it was only that he temporarily forgot his father's secret. But there was something more. Just for a moment, for one second, he felt fierce.

His father took the mask from his hands. "Careful there. You like this one?"

Rafe nodded.

"This is a Dan mask, from the Ivory Coast. It was-and maybe still is—used in their ceremonies to talk to the spirit realm."

"The spirit realm?"

"Yes. Every tree and rock has soul, a spirit. The forest is full of spirits."

Almost immediately, Rafe's world changed. His mind was filled with swirling shapes hiding among the mossy trees of a rainforest that dripped with shiny insects and technicolor birds. Insubstantial shapes that, when they coalesced, became black people. People with skin like his, noses and lips like his. *Angels and elves and ghosts that looked like him.* Rafe thought only white people had spirit realms, enchanted forests, creatures with shining golden hair and blue eyes. Every game, every book, and every movie had them. He would have to explore this unknown world.

His father must have seen something in his face, some expression. “You really like this mask, don’t you?”

“Yeah,” Rafe managed.

Pops smiled. “It’s yours. I know that I’ve missed your birthdays. And I’m really proud that you won that scholarship. Consider this—”

Rafe didn’t let him finish. He hugged his dad. Not only for the gift, but also for the pain he was going through. The hug was Rafe’s gift, his secret message to his father’s pain.

The barbershop was on the lower level of the mall. It smelled, as all barbershops do, of pomade, powder, and oil. The checkerboard floor was grimy, the corners filled with hills of shorn hair. Three young men lounged in chairs, reading newspapers or texting on their smartphones. An older man in a white coat stopped sweeping one of the hair-hills, and smiled.

“Hey, Sam!” said the white-coated man. “How are you? This your kid?”

“Yes. This is Rafael.”

“Put it there,” said the barber, extending his hand. Rafe squeezed the papery hand.

“Listen, Ben, he has to get a haircut. The new school he’s going to has a dress code.”

Ben nodded. “Tyrone? Why don’t you help this young gentleman here?”

A tall, skinny man of about twenty slowly stood up from the barber chair, and motioned for Rafe to sit. Once he was wrapped in a white sheet with his head sticking out, Tyrone asked him how much he wanted cut off. Rafe told him the whole thing.

"Damn," said Tyrone. "That school ain't playing around. How long did it take you to grow your dreads?"

"Two years," Rafe mumbled. *Two long years. Every lock was precious.* "I have no choice."

Tyrone made a tsking sound. "You gotta do what you gotta do." Tyrone grabbed scissors from his work station, and spun Rafe toward the mirror. Were scissor blades ever so shiny? *Snick*. One lock dropped from his scalp. It was a black one. *Snick*. Another went, whorled with the lightest auburn threads. *Snick, snick, snick*. They fell like leaves.

I will not cry.

That would only make it worse. Tears falling down among the leaves. When Tyrone spun the chair around to work on the front dreads, Rafe saw his severed hair on the floor. They were lifeless pieces of himself, just lying there, against the floor.

CHAPTER THREE
SIDESHOW

Hunter," said the red-haired kid, and offered a clammy hand to Rafe. The kid was a little taller than Rafe. His face was covered in orange-brown freckles, slightly darker than the orange crew cut he sported. Like Rafe, he was dressed in the same outfit—gray pants, white shirt, burgundy blazer. Hunter didn't smile, which was fine—Rafe didn't feel like smiling either. For one thing, it was 7:30 in the morning. After a season of getting up at 10:00, it was hard to focus. And for another, Rafe needed to focus, to get his bearings.

Hunter said, "Feel free to ask me anything. Our Lady can be confusing the first couple of weeks."

"Thanks."

The first place they went was to the lockers. When they left the office, Rafe noticed that the empty halls had filled up. Boys in burgundy paced and milled in the hallway, in the eaves of the classrooms. As he and Hunter passed, some of them stopped talking and stared at him. *The New Kid Glare.* Sizing him up. Their faces were so many different shades of pale: from almost transparent white, where you could see the blood and the veins, to peach, to apple, to beige, to almost-but-not-quite brown. Eyes of blue and green flickered past.

Rafe and Hunter went down one hall, then

another, until they came to a bank of lockers that looked the same as any other.

"What's your number?" Hunter asked. He checked his watch.

Rafe told him, and struggled with the combination for a good three minutes. He always had trouble with combinations—some things never changed. When it finally popped open and he put his stuff in, a bell rang. The halls filled suddenly, students spilling from previously invisible places. He saw Hunter talking to a group of other boys. Hunter was a lot more laid back with them, laughing and less business-like.

As Rafe approached the group of four boys surrounding the redhead, he overheard the tail end of a conversation.

"Yeah, I was early. Had to help one of the scholarship kids get settled," Hunter said.

Rafe stood back from them; he hated being talked about. It made his skin itch.

"Hey, Rafe," said Hunter, "Lemme introduce you to some people."

All four boys had brown hair and brown eyes. They could have been brothers, and their names—Simon, Will, John, and Pete—all got jumbled together. One of them said, "Hey, man," and another gave him a fist bump.

The one with glasses—maybe Pete—said, "Welcome to Our Shady Lady."

Rafe laughed. It was good to know someone in this sea of whiteness. Except—he saw a brown face drift by. The black kid did't give him *The New Kid Glare*—he ignored him. Or Rafe imagined that he was ignored; he wasn't sure. A moment later, another brown face walked by—probably a Latino kid. He, at least, gave a half-nod. Then another bell rang and the various groups in the hall dispersed. Hunter took Rafe to homeroom.

There were a couple of other kids already sitting in the room. They sat at desks that were arranged in a circle, with name tents on them. Rafe found his. It was next to a boy who reminded him of an owl, with his bowlcut, light-brown hair and round Harry Potter glasses. He even had an owlish name—Theodore Braxton. Rafe sat across from Brian Oglivy, a fat kid with frizzy blond hair and a penchant for chewing his nails. Gradually, the other twenty kids trickled in and took their places. All avoided looking at each other.

At least that's one good thing. Most of the kids don't know each other. They're all The New Kid here.

In walked Mr. O'Connell, looking not much older than the rest of them, though he'd grown a completely awkward-looking mustache and beard combo. He grinned goofily at Rafe. Rafe tried to look away without appearing to be an asshole.

As Mr. O'Connell spoke, silly thoughts filled Rafe's head. *What kind of a name is Angus? Sounds like a hamburger. And Angus O'Connell = Anus O'Connell.* He stopped himself from laughing just as Hamburger Anus told them to bow their heads in prayer.

Rafe and his mother had gone to church the previous day. She told him it was both to get right with God, since they'd been away from the church for so long, and to prepare him for the intense religious instruction at Our Lady of the Woods. His last day of freedom was spent stuffing himself into stiff clothing and a necktie like a noose. A last-minute heat wave hit the city, so waiting for the bus was uncomfortable.

Thankfully, Imani Faith Temple was air-conditioned. It might have been a little too air-conditioned; Rafe's sweat chilled quickly and became cold. He knew that Hell was hot, like the outside was. Was Heaven overly cold, like here? It smelled like a church inside—that peculiar mixture of wood soap, old stone, felt banners, candle wax, and perfume. In the vestibule, Rafe saw some old Sunday-school compatriots, DeAndra and Victor. Like him, they were shivering in starched clothing. Did grown-ups never get uncomfortable in their clothing? Some of his mother's church friends greeted her—"Nice to see you, Sister Ursele." She told these quasi-strangers about Rafe's scholarship (cue for the polite smile) and her own mysterious ailments (too much information, in Rafe's opinion). Rafe noticed that it was mostly women who gathered for the service—women and their sons, and occasionally a husband or two. All of the women, including his mother, wore a hat of some kind. His mother's was wide brimmed and made of some gray mesh material. Others had flowers on them—plastic roses or azaleas or pansies that moved in the air-conditioned breeze.

The sounds of the pipe organ, both throaty and metallic, thrummed through the building, silencing conversation. The congregation moved into the worship hall with its dark wooden pews and wide stone avenues. The stage was lit with a warm brightness. The stainedglass windows cast pools of color on every surface. Rafe glanced at the windows. He saw some of the classic Bible stories—there, in green and gold and brown glass was Noah's Ark. A dove made of milky opaque glass carried a branch to Noah's welcoming hands. Noah's brown hands and face. Another stained-glass image showed Mary cradling the Christ child, their bronzy-brown skins against a background of gas-blue light. Their halos burned with the light of the sun. Rafe thought about Our Lady of Concrete, stone-faced Galadriel in her blood-red room, and how different she was from this dark-skinned Mary. Our Lady's Madonna was pure and mysterious, an aloof elf-queen. This glowing Madonna was open and welcoming.

The stage began to fill up. Behind the podium, which was emblazoned with a squat cross, choir members floated in; they wore black robes covered with deep purple mantles that had the same squat cross etched in gold thread. The metal pipes of the organ gleamed like monstrous teeth at the back of the stage. Segments of colored light from the windows splashed the stage. Rafe's father would call all this pomp and circumstance a bunch of B.S., black folks led like lambs to the slaughter that was the white man's religion. Rafe's father believed that putting a black mask over a white face did nothing to absolve its poisonous nature. Religion was one of the many things that divided Rafe's parents. Sometimes, Rafe even wondered how they managed to stop arguing long enough to conceive him. But sitting here, in such a saturated world, it was hard not to feel holiness. Holiness rose from the deep voice of the organ, and the massed voices joined that sea-deep sound.

The bishop was a giant of a man—he could have easily been a wide receiver. He was dark-skinned, with white hair and had the sonorous tones of James Earl Jones. When Rafe was bored with the prayers, he imaged Darth Vader leading the congregation. After the service, which lasted about an hour, people went to the church basement for weak pink punch and stale cookies. Rafe's mother got reacquainted with some old church friends, while Rafe stood by the door, nursing a cup of sweet punch.

DeAndra came up to him. "Hey, Rafael," she said. He didn't bother updating her with his nickname; his full name was his church-name and would probably never change. "Heard you got into Our Lady of the Woods. Are you excited?"

"Sort of." *Not really.*

"You cut your hair." She reached up and touched it. Rafe felt her fingers on his scalp. It tingled. "I thought it was cute."

Cute? Rafe hoped he wasn't blushing. *What should I say? Thank you?* He decided to ignore the comment—that seemed safest. "They made me," he replied.

"What do you mean?"

They were interrupted by Victor. He and Rafe were the same age, but Victor was taller. His skin was smoother and clear, and even through his blazer, Rafe could make out his muscles sliding beneath the fabric. Victor smiled, with perfect teeth, as shiny as the organ's pipes. He gave Rafe a big hug, and Rafe could smell him—deodorant, Axe spray, a whiff of underarm sweat. "How you doin', man?" Victor asked, and Rafe tingled like when DeAndra touched him. He pulled back. "Been a while since I saw you."

"Yeah, well. You know how it is. And Mom's been sick."

"Sorry to hear that, man." Even Victor's voice was deep, compared to the squeak of Rafe's.

The three of them caught up—DeAndra was still in sixth grade, while Victor was starting junior high, like he was, but at Parks—the school Rafe would have gone to if he hadn't won the scholarship. Not for the first time did he wish that he was going to Parks instead of that tight-assed school. Before Rafe's mother collected him, he got DeAndra and Victor's email addresses and phone numbers, even though he knew that he would never call them. Just knowing that he *could* call them, if he wanted to, was somehow enough.

Rafe and his mother walked out of the cool heaven of the air-conditioned church into the blistering hell of outside. They didn't say anything as they waited for the bus—why waste breath when breathing itself caused you to sweat? When the bus finally trundled up, Rafe had already removed his blazer, and his mother's hair had begun to frizz out. The mostly empty bus was lukewarm, but better than what was outside.

"That was nice," Rafe's mother said, after they'd cooled off slightly.

"I guess."

The road was particularly bumpy; Imani Faith was on a street that had seen better days.

Rafe's mother said, "I saw you talking to DeAndra Sommers. She grew up nice."

Rafe supposed DeAndra had 'grown up nice'—

she'd let her hair grow out and it was a light brown and curled. The dress she wore was simple and black, but she had a waist now, and wasn't a string bean anymore. Rafe tried to focus on her and forget that he had noticed Victor more. The slight protrusion of his Adam's apple that slid up and down his throat, the phantom whiskers on his upper lip.

"Yeah," he said, a moment too late. Not that it mattered; his mother wasn't really paying attention to him. She had a faraway look, as if she didn't see the business district flowing past the bus windows.

"I knew going to church was the right thing to do," she said. "Great things are in store for the family."

Rafe immediately thought of his father and the wreck of a van he called home. Chinese food boxes and empty cans of tuna...

"You know how I know, Rafael?"

Rafe shook his head.

"God told me."

Rafe didn't say anything. What was there to say?

"Last night, I had the hardest time getting to sleep. My nerves were acting up again. It's like they're on fire, every strand burning. So I got up and read a little. But that didn't help, not at all. I was going to take something, but the drugs don't really seem to help either. I decided to get up and make some hot milk—that seems to help, sometimes."

Rafe's mother kept talking as the bus jostled them. "I went to the kitchen, and of course, we were out of milk. But before I closed the fridge door, I knew that I wasn't alone. But I wasn't scared. Remember when you were little, and you'd fall asleep in one place and wake in another? You were disoriented and confused, but it was all right, because you could *sense* that your parents were around. And as long as they were around, everything was safe. Well, that feeling filled me up."

Rafe's mother paused for a moment. He wasn't sure what look she had on her face.

"I closed the fridge, and slowly turned around. When I was about your age, my grandmother had a cabinet in her house filled with the most wonderful glass angels. They were so delicate and some of their wings were lightly colored–just a hint of blue, a bit of pink. I saw one, life-sized, standing in the kitchen with me. I could hardly make it out–it was transparent, like glass, but *oh,* the wings were *amazing*. The pair of them was largethey spread out and almost filled the kitchen. They were shaded with the palest purple tint—I think you'd call it lilac."

At this point, they were near their stop—maybe five minutes away. Rafe's mother's eyes glowed with a weird shine, as if she were sick and her eyeballs were sweating. For some reason, Rafe thought about the mask that his father had given him a couple of weeks ago, the empty eyeholes that seemed to be looking out. Rafe broke her gaze, looked around the bus. He was relieved it was mostly empty. There was one man who looked like he might be listening, but Rafe couldn't be sure.

"It was beautiful. And I mean *it*. I didn't know if it was male or female. I am not sure that things like that matter when you stand in front of the Lord. When the angel spoke to me, I heard it in my head. It sent me waves of love, waves of love that took away my pain and fear. It told me that things were going to be all right for us, that God had blessed us. Then it told me to follow it. I did, and it led me to your room. We watched you sleeping, the angel and I. The angel's wings shimmered with the lilac color as it blessed you, Rafael. Praise Jesus!"

This last "praise Jesus" was a little loud, and the one passenger who pretended not to listen definitely turned his head. Rafe didn't know what to say, so he took his mother's hand. She squeezed it back. Her grip was strong this time, and as they walked back to their building, she had an actual spring to her step. She spent the rest of the day doing Sunday chores—laundry, straightening upwhile singing. Rafe's mother had a lovely voice, but her nthusiastic singing caused her to go off key a few times. She laughed when this happened.

"Praise Jesus," said Anus O'Connell, signaling the end of the prayer. The boys all murmured their amens. They spent the rest of the hour getting to know each other—their names, what schools they came from, their favorite hobbies. When Rafe gave his brief, no-morethan-three-sentences bio, just like the other boys (Garvey Elementary, city native, comic books), O'Connell butted in.

"I would also like to add that Rafe one of our Toussaint Scholars," he said, with his clueless, goofy grin. "We're lucky to have him."

The other boys leered at him. Yes, *leered*. Rafe saw eyes brand him *Teacher's Pet* and *Suck Up*. He smiled weakly and wished he had the balls to act up in class. But he couldn't. It was the first day, and besides, both of his parents were united in wanting him to succeed. An angel had visited his mom; he couldn't afford to screw up. The bell rang, ending the awkward moment. As Rafe left the classroom, O'Connell gently patted his back, like they were the best of friends. Rafe did his best not to flinch.

Since it was the first day of school, all of the students filed into the auditorium for some kind of ceremony. They all sat by grade, with the seniors up front. It struck Rafe for the first time that he was in an all-male school. The sound of audience chatter was somehow different. Maybe it was only the absence of higher voices. It also smelled different—sweatier, muskier. He kind of missed the girls, even though they could be a pain in the ass.

I thought your hair was cute. DeAndra's voice replayed, along with the tingle as her hand touched his now-shorn head.

A hush fell over the student body as Angus O'Connell took the stage. "Please bow your heads in prayer."

Rafe thought about his mother's angel as the prayer droned on. *Was he—or she—watching over him, with a glass face and lilac wings?* The thought was both enthralling and creepy. His mother had basically described some kind of beautiful monster, like you'd see in a Tim Burton movie, one that was sparkling and gorgeous, just before it revealed a mouthful of glass teeth.

The rest of the program was overlong and boring, like the TV news. Blah blah, *this new teacher*. Blah, blah, *this year will be exciting*. Blah, blah. Rafe zoned out, like many of the other students. By the time the assembly was over, everyone, including the teachers and staff, were restless. At least there would be a cook-out, outside on the blacktop.

Outside, cliques formed immediately among the older students, in continental drifts. The seventh graders, by contrast, were islands on the sea of tar. The September heat wave blasted the area, but everyone waited in line in their stifling blazers to get a hot dog or hamburger. As Rafe moved closer and closer to the tent where the burgers and hot dogs were—it was at least as hot inside the tent as Mustafar, the volcano planet where Obi Wan Kenobi struck down Anakin/Darth Vader—he saw a group of Latino and black cooks, sweating in the shimmering heat. The other boys ignored the workers.

Rafe's mother could have be serving this food: she was a cafeteria worker. The thought of these lily-white boys being served by her almost made Rafe lose his appetite. The thing that *did* make him lose his appetite was the charred, shriveled burger on the supermarket bun. It was a lump of greasy coal.

"Looks like a turd," someone behind him said.

Rafe turned, and saw Tomás—from his old school.

"Aw, man. I didn't know you made it in here, too!" Rafe was tempted to drop the turd-burger and hug Tomás. He didn't—that would look too gay.

"What did you think—you were the only smart nigga at Garvey?"

Rafe laughed. The two of them left the sweltering tent and found a retaining wall to sit on and eat their inedible food.

Tomás said, between bites of his pink hot dog, striped with grillmarks, "I see they made you cut your hair, too."

"Man," Rafe said. At Garvey, Tomás sported a frizzy 'fro, one that earned him the nickname "Sideshow," after Sideshow Bob from *The Simpsons*. Now, like Rafe, his head was shorn close to the skull.

"Guess there's no point in calling you Sideshow anymore," Rafe said.

"Damn right. That pansy-ass preacher dude told me: 'Listen—what is it you people say to each other—listen, bro; Our Lady of the *White* Woods has a dress code. It's not, as you people say, whack to have long hair.'"

Tomás's impression of O'Connell was spot-on, from the awkward, nasal voice to the air-quote gestures. Both Rafe and Sideshow cracked up. Rafe told Tomás his nickname for the vicar—Anus O'Connell—and more laughter erupted. So much laughter spilled out that a sour-faced teacher glanced in their direction, as well as a few curious students.

When they got ahold of themselves, Rafe whispered to Sideshow, "They all look at us like someone farted."

"They ain't used to seeing The Help at their school," said Tomás, and they both had to suppress more giggling.

The pitiful lunch hour went by quickly. When the bell finally rang, Rafe no longer felt so alone. He was even *happy*.

Maybe his mother's weird lilac-winged angel *was* watching over him.

CHAPTER FOUR
DARK ENERGY

The television was on when Rafe got back home from school—he could hear the broadcast voices through the door. That meant that his mother had stayed home today. This morning, she'd had a flare-up of nerve pain and stayed in, rather than walking with him to the bus stop.

"Hey, Mom," he said, opening the door. She wasn't sitting in her usual spot in front of the TV, and the kitchenette was empty. A TV doctor, Oz or Phil, chatted to a studio audience. Rafe put his book bag down—it was a lot heavier than the book bag he'd brought home from elementary school. The textbooks he'd gotten in class were Bible-sized tomes. But he liked carrying them, in spite of that. Or maybe because they were tomes. For one thing, the books at Our Lady were new, no handme-downs. The new matte-page smell drifted up when he opened them. The glue that held them together hadn't cracked. They were unmarred by notes and highlighter pens. And the illustrations were enthralling: the algebra equations, the scientific diagrams, the tiny text of the history book all beckoned to him. Plus, he had a thumbdrive full of homework and examples in one of the book bag's numerous compartments.

The first few days at Our Lady weren't so bad after all. For one thing, all of Rafe's fellow classmates were basically in the same boat he was—the lowest in the pecking order, and clueless. They were all new to the school, even if the bulk of them had come from the same feeder school—St. Agnes—and therefore knew each other. Best of all, though, Sideshow was there with his quips. They shared two classes together.

Rafe's mother came out of his room. She smiled. "How was your day, baby?"

"It wasn't too bad. I have a lotta homework, though. Just the first week. How are you doing?"

She turned down the TV. "You know, I was feeling pretty lousy. Then, I started praying, and you know what? By the afternoon, I was feeling pretty good."

"That's great."

"Praise Jesus. He's good to us." That strange fire burned in her eyes—the angel-fire.

Rafe said, "He sure is." He hoped he sounded convincing. "Well, I should start on my homework."

Rafe's mother smiled, and told him that dinner would be ready in about an hour.

Rafe's bedroom was a retro-fitted walk-in closet; his desk was one of the few remaining shelves. With the daybed on the opposite side, there was barely enough room for the folding chair. Light—and now the rented laptop—got their power from an extension cord that snaked outside the room. The one good thing about Rafe's bedroom was that the door was pretty thick; once you closed it, very few sounds could make it in, except from the small window that faced the street.

Because it was so small, Rafe noticed the addition to the room immediately. Right next to the laptop, the glass angel stood glaring at him. Her wings were folded, as were her hands. For some reason, Rafe thought it was creepy. He saw Stations of the Cross and sad-eyed saints all day at Our Lady. He didn't want them with him at home, too. Some impulse made him turn to face the other image staring at him—the Dan mask. It, too, watched over him. Rafe laughed—it was like a face-off. *Angel vs. Mask*. Which one would get to bless him? It was silly, though. Both were inanimate objects. All the same, Rafe moved the angel so that it wasn't facing him when he turned on his computer.

About an hour later, his mother knocked on the door. Dinner was baked chicken, frozen string beans, powdered mashed potatoes, and a side of sweet tea from a mix. The prayer before they ate lasted longer than usual. Rafe only really noticed his mother going on and on about how merciful He was because he was so hungry.

After the prayer, Rafe spoke. He didn't know what compelled him to say "Thanks for the angel," even though he thought it was tacky and a little creepy. It looked like it was ordered from one of those ads from a ladies' magazine—the ones that sold commemorative plates honoring John F. Kennedy or Obama.

His mother beamed. "My grandmother had one that was similar. After I had been healed, I went to Imani."

Imani Faith had a small, almost always empty gift shop that sold rosary beads, incense, candles, and 3D pictures of Mary and Jesus. The glass angels had just come in. "I wanted to get all of them. But of course, I could only get one. Rafe, stop picking your teeth. It's rude."

Rafe would have to endure the piece of chicken skin caught between his teeth until after dinner. "Why'd you put it in my room?" That came out a bit whinier than he meant it to.

"Don't you like it?"

"Yes." *No,* he thought.

"I thought it might brighten your room. It's so empty. And that god-awful mask your father gave you, right above your bed..."

"What's wrong with that?"

Rafe's mother looked at her plate, moved some green beans around. "I can't put my finger on it. But it has some dark—energy."

Rafe dropped his fork. "Dark energy? Like it's evil or something?"

"You know what? Forget about it. It was a lovely gesture, for your father to give you something nice. How is he doing?"

Rafe's annoyance at his mother died down. Images of his father's "home"—the van—flashed before him. He'd spoken to his father on Saturday. At least Pops still had a cell phone.

"He's doing fine. He said that business is really picking up."

"Did he, now." Rafe's mother had her lie-detection expression on her face: a teardrop-shaped depression formed in the middle of her forehead and her right eyebrow went up slightly.

"Yeah, that's what he said." *Screw this war between Mom and Dad.* "I think we should have him over for dinner sometime."

Her expression changed immediately to one of shock? She laughed, a derisive laugh. “Ha! That’ll never happen.” It was a nasty, even *bitchy*, thing to say. But it sounded like the old Ursele who had been missing for a while, and that made him happy for a moment. Where had this frail holy-roller come from? And what had she done with his mother? It was as if his real mother was buried somewhere deep inside. The old Ursele had been made of steel. The new Ursele was as fragile as that glass angel.

They finished dinner and his mother watched a little TV while Rafe washed up. Afterward, Rafe went back to his room and finished his homework. Italicized equations filled his head. X and N and other new notations were confusing but fascinating at the same time. It was like learning another language. When he finished, he surfed the web a bit. He Googled the term “dark energy” just for the hell of it.

“Dark energy” was a cosmic term, related to “dark matter.” It was the stuff that space was made of, energy that flowed through a dark void. Rafe fell into a data-hole for a moment, reading about quasars, brown dwarfs, and black holes. His inner nerd woke up. Then his mother knocked on his bedroom door. Which version of her would be behind the door?

“You still up?” she asked. She was in her nightgown, and her hair was wrapped up in some kind of turban.

“I’m going to bed in a moment.”

She kissed him, went to her bedroom, and closed the door. Five minutes later—after brushing his teeth—Rafe lay in his room. Lights from the street danced on the ceiling. The white bars of passing headlights, the blue and red kaleidoscope of police lights. Rafe considered getting up and pulling down the shades, but he didn't. Maybe because he was lazy and it involved standing on a chair at an awkward angle. But that wasn't it, not completely. He was mesmerized by the lights on the walls and the way they prismed through the glass angel. Colors sparked through her form. She absorbed light and sent it back in shimmering rays. Maybe an angel *did* visit Rafe's mom that night. Who knew?

The Dan mask hung just above his head, eyelessly staring at the glass angel. Some of her refracted light splashed on its wooden face. *Did it have dark energy hidden in its halo of shells?* Rafe reached up and touched the face. It was warm, like skin.

Before he went to jail, Rafe's father and Rafe would always hang out on the weekends. His father lived in the 'burbs, in a studio garden apartment that was a dump. It was sparsely furnished. The kitchen had the world's smallest oven. There was a futon and a folding table with a couple of chairs. All of that didn't matter, though. Rafe's dad had a huge, 24-inch TV with an old Wii console. Days with Pops always included pizza from the super greasy, super good place a couple of blocks away, soda so concentrated with sugar that his teeth hurt, and games or movies on the Wii. Every now and then, Pops got serious. He'd been studying about African art and folklore.

"You read all those trashy sci-fi and fantasy books," Pops said once, "about white people in the future or white people's magical past."

"They're not trashy. Not all of them, anyway."

"All right, you're right. I like some of them, too. I read Asimov and *Dune* when I was a little older than you and loved them. The thing is, we—black people—we have our own myths and fantasy worlds..."

And then Pops began to tell him some of the stories about a mischievous spider or a black mermaid who was fiercer than Ariel was in *The Little Mermaid*.

Just then, a car light illuminated the angel in Rafe's room. It flared, silver-white, traced with the palest mauve color. The glass angel had its own energy, brighter than the mask's, but it still creeped him out. Which was worse: the eyeless mask or the strange light behind his mother's eyes?

CHAPTER FIVE
LEGOLAS

Garvey Elementary never had a proper physical education class. There were occasional kickball games in the spring, but the school had neither the grounds or the money for a sustained class. So this was literally Rafe's first time in a gymnasium. It was huge, cavernous, with a blond lacquered floor, basketball hoops, and bleachers. Sleeping digital scoreboards were mounted high on a wall. The floor had the Our Lady of the Woods logo—a stylized burgundy O with clasped hands in the center. The cinderblocks were painted a bright, institutional yellow color, midway between margarine and mustard. It smelled of old sweat and Lysol. The boys were all lined up in grey sweatsuits with Our Lady of the Woods burgundy lettering on them. In a locker room that had bright, shiny new lockers and freshly grouted shower tiles, the boys all changed quickly without looking at each other. In spite of that, Rafe caught glimpses of body parts: bared chests marked with birthmarks and scars, puffy nipples, bulges of fat. He was sure that at least some kids looked at his skin, with its tendency to be dry and ashy, or the stubborn triangle of curly hair that had sprouted in the middle of his chest. The furtive changing was over quickly, and the students all lined up like military cadets taking orders.

The coach sauntered out in a shiny black tracksuit. He introduced himself as Mr. Loomis. His dirty brown-blond hair looked like an upside-down bowl on his wide brow. A thick, sculpted mustache curled above his thick lips, giving him a kind of pervy look—didn't all those pedophile creeps on *To Catch a Predator* have big moustaches? Mr. Loomis's voice boomed like a TV sports announcer's. Rafe found himself listening for the cicada-thick wall of cheers that usually accompanied such a voice.

"When I call your name, get in alphabetical order against the wall. You think you can handle that?"

When Mr. Loomis got to Rafael Fannen, the coach remarked, "You're no Lebron." Several boys Rafe couldn't see laughed. Rafe knew that he was short for his age, but that was the sort of remark he would have expected from another student, not a teacher. *Chickenhead*, he thought. But the hot flare of shame passed when, a couple of names later, Loomis said something about a fat kidCharles Seeley—that got other boys laughing. "Seeley, eh? More like Sea Lion. We're gonna have to work on that, son." Rafe checked Seeley's face, and was happy to see that it was stoic, that he hadn't broken down. That kid would probably be called Sea Lion for the rest of the eighth grade.

Loomis made a mess of an Indian kid's name—"Mahalala Ringadingdong," he said, laughing at his own joke. The Indian kid—with too-big Harry Potter glassesscuttled quickly across the floor, with his head down. No one else laughed. They all understood Loomis was a jerk. *So much for being a Christian school*, Rafe thought.

More names, interspersed with insults. Toby

Nelson stepped forward when his name was called. Loomis said, “Aren’t you a pretty boy? We’ll call you Movie Star.”

“Jealous?”

Rafe had been staring straight and center—he had no desire to hear Loomis’s lame attempts at humor, but he, along with the rest of the boys, all turned toward the boy who challenged the coach. He *was* a pretty boy. He was slim, with sinewy muscles just beginning to sprout. He stood a few inches taller than most of the other eighth graders. His hair was a rich golden color, like wheat, and he had blue, blue eyes, the color of some secret sea. He reminded Rafe of Legolas, from The *Lord of the Rings*—he had an arrogant, elfin glamour.

The coach looked up from his clipboard and glared at Toby. “Excuse me?” he asked, his voice low and dangerous.

Everyone waited to hear what would happen next. Toby just smiled at Loomis and took his place in line. But the smile was more than a mere curling of the lips. It was the flash of a dagger, a gauntlet thrown down. Loomis glowered at the boy, like a Balrog. After a moment, Loomis went back to roll call. No one after Toby was insulted or given a new nickname.

“Damn, the water is cold!”

“Like a witch’s titty.”

Rafe and Seeley were the last ones to enter the maze of the showers. Rafe waited until Seeley removed his clothes before he took off his own. Seeing how un-selfconscious the larger boy was—

with his pasty pale skin marked by angry red stretch marks—gave Rafe some courage. Nude boys, standing under frigid showers that reeked of chlorine, laughed and chattered. As they walked by, a few boys called out, "Here comes Sea Lion!" Seeley ignored them. Rafe had never been naked before this many strangers. He tried his best not to look at the wet flesh of the others and also ignored the awkward flopping of his own private parts. Toby had gone to the showers first, unashamed. His white skin didn't have a blemish on it. His nipples were bright pink and dead center of his pectorals. Rafe looked away quickly, afraid of—what? The only free shower spot was next to Toby.

Needles of ice rained down on Rafe's skin. It reminded him of when the hot water heater at the apartment building broke for a week a couple of winters past. It was liquid frostbite. Rafe gasped.

"You okay there, little buddy?"

Through the curtain of water, Rafe saw Toby. His hair was wet gold, and his eyes were as icy blue as the water felt. His pale skin was stippled with gooseflesh. He turned away and pressed the canister of liquid soap, which was as pink as his nipples. Toby worked the pink soap into a white lather and sluiced it over his body, across his chest, beneath his balls, between his ass cheeks.

No homo.

Rafe turned away. He focused on the cold water pounding on his skin. He rubbed the astringent pink soap over his own body and faced the shower wall until the world became tile and grout. He focused on cleaning himself. There were no washcloths, just towels, so he had to use his hands to scrub the stink off himself. His body ached from the exertion of quick sprints and laps around the gym. All in all, he had done pretty well. The Indian kid, Mahalala, had to stop due to a mild asthma attack. Loomis shouted, "Ramadama Dingdong is out!" Seeley stopped after three laps and then began walking the laps. Rafe managed to complete five laps—the same as Toby.

Butterflies fluttered in Rafe's stomach. Their wings rustled and stirred, wings the color of lilacs. They crawled over each other, in two directions. One, toward the burning flame of his heart; the other, toward his groin. They crept up and down his nerves. Rafe avoided washing his junk. Maybe if he ignored it, the tingling feeling would go away. But it didn't. It grew and bloomed. It glowed, like embers, like a Balrog.

No homo.

Toby had run next to Rafe for a while. Each muscle slid beneath Toby's smooth ivory skin. Even under gray sweats, Rafe could sense the flex and tension of each muscle. What would Toby feel like, his cold skin beneath Rafe's fingers? He saw an elf, crouching, notching an arrow in a long bow. The elf waited a beat and then sent the arrow out into the air, into the dark heart of an orc.

No homo.

There was only one thing to do to kill the lilac-winged butterflies fluttering in Rafe's stomach. He pressed the soap dispenser. Pink as poison, the soap lay in the palm of his hand. It diluted under the steady stream of icy water. A few bubbles rose and burst, quick, pink deaths.

No homo.

Rafe threw the soap into his eyes. The sting was immediate, blinding. He blinked his eyes rapidly—and with each blink, one of the butterflies died.

Legolas faded. Nude, white flesh kissed pink by cold water vanished from his mind.

Each wing-beat stilled, silenced by the insecticide of the pink soap. Thoraxes drank the poison of his pain and died.

❖

"What happened to your eye, man?"

Rafe and Sideshow sat at the end of a long table of fellow eighth graders. Each kid had a bright orange tray with a plate of steaming slop on it. One mound was brown and was either meatloaf or Salisbury steak, and another mound was lard-white—presumably, mashed potatoes. A tiny bowl of watery lima beans and clown-red cubes of gelatin were also on the tray. Rafe poked one of the Jello-cubes—it was topped with something that was a little too stiff to be real whipped cream.

"I got some soap in my eye," he said. "Does it look too bad?"

Sideshow said, "You just look like you smoked a blunt."

Rafe gave a half-hearted snicker and started on the Salisbury-loaf. It tasted terrible. Underneath the rubbery brown sauce, the meat was gray. He pushed his plate away.

"It looks like roadkill," Rafe said.

"Aw, man. Now you made me lose my appetite. You think they scraped a possum up outside and threw it into the stew pot? 'This will make fine eating for the pretties!'" Tomás imitated a horror-movie witch, complete with cackle.

Rafe laughed, even as he winced—his left eye still stung. He still couldn't believe what he'd done—now he thought it was a major stupid move. It wasn't like he'd had a boner when he'd seen Toby naked. An image of water and soap sliding down the peach and white body popped into his head, unbidden. Shame stirred—it moved beneath his scalp, made it itch. He also saw Victor, as tall as Toby, same lithe frame—Rafe blinked and rode the wave of pain.

"Are you crying?"

"Shut up," Rafe said.

A couple of tables over, Toby sat with a group of other boys. He laughed at some joke. Rafe saw how his Adam's apple moved in his throat, the white of his teeth, the way light glinted off of his blue, blue eyes.

"What are you looking at?" Sideshow interrupted him. Sideshow turned around in an awkward way and tried to suss out where Rafe was looking. "You looking at that white faggot?"

Sideshow said that a little too loudly. Several boys at their table looked up. Rafe buried his head in his hands.

"Could you be a little more *obvious*?" Jeez, Tomás could be so very ghetto.

Sideshow didn't seem to feel shame of any kind. He just gawked at Toby. "What about him?"

"Sideshow, turn around," Rafe whispered. *Turn around before he sees you looking at him.*

Sideshow obeyed. Rafe told him about Toby standing up to the gym teacher.

"That Loomis guy sounds like a jerk," Sideshow said at the end of the story.

"He really is. And he looks like a perv."

Seeley walked by them just then, finished with his lunch. He moved past the table where Toby sat.

Toby stopped talking and said, "Hey, Sea Lion!" Seeley continued to the counter to bus his tray. He gave no indication that he'd heard Toby.

"Sea Lion! I was talking to you!"

There was still no response as the large kid left the orange tray on a conveyor belt.

Toby and some of his friends started to make barking noises and flapped their hands as if they were flippers. Seeley walked out of the cafeteria, and Toby's friends laughed like cartoon hyenas.

Sideshow said, "Looks like your boy is a bit of an a-hole, too."

❖

"Latin is like the Force," said Mr. Dubois. "It is the glue that binds our language. Surrounds the language, bolsters it, flows through it. 'Luminous beings are we.'"

Rafe laughed—this guy was so corny! Mr. Dubois was short and rotund, with a bowling-ball belly. His dark brown hair seemed to be composed completely of cowlicks, and he had the thick muttonchops of a nineteenth-century British dude.

"Ah! I see I've managed to make our Moorish friend here laugh."

Moorish? WTF did that mean?

Dubois persisted: "I would wager to guess you are a fan of the wisdom of Yoda."

Actually, Rafe was not particularly a fan of *Star Wars*, and the small green imp thing that was Yoda creeped him out.

"Not really," Rafe mumbled, self-consciously. He could feel all the eyes on him.

"Not a *Star Wars* fan? Fie! I suppose *Harry Potter* is more your speed... Mr. Fannen."

Rafe nodded cautiously. *Where was this going?* "That's just as well. Mr. Potter and the denizens of his magical world base their spells on Latinate or, really, *Latin-esque* verbiage. While we won't be able to repel a Dementor or levitate, Latin does have a magical... essence. It is Romantic." He pronounced each syllable of that word, and rolled the R dramatically. "Latin is the blueprint language, the ur-text..."

"No, it's not." Everyone turned to the source of the new voice. It was Mahalala who, ironically, looked like a brown version of Harry Potter. "I mean, all language doesn't come from Latin."

Dubois spun on his heels. "Our Eastern friend here is quite correct. I did not mean to suggest that Latin is the *mater* of all *lingua*. Here, in the Occident, though, most major languages—French, Spanish, Italian and, of course, English—can trace their lineage to Latin."

"I'm not Eastern," said Mahalala. "I'm from Cleveland."

Everyone laughed at that—even Mahalala.

"That Dubois is so goofy," said Rafe. Class had just let out and students spilled into the linoleum river of the hallway.

Mahalala flinched. When he saw it was Rafe, he seemed to relax. "Yeah. He was kind of annoying. A know-it-all. What's your next class?"

"History."

"Mine's English—right next door."

The two of them moved into the crush of rowdy boys. Only a week in, and certain cliques had already formed. The older classmen mostly ignored the eighth gradersthey might as well have been invisible. Lockers opened, revealing pictures of rock stars and hot babes taped to the inside of doors, along with the stacks of books. They overheard some of conversations. The phrase "that's so gay" showed up in more than three of them. Not that Rafe was keeping count.

"He called me Moorish. Like when he called you Eastern."

Mahalala laughed. His teeth were bright white and gleamed in contrast to his dark skin. "That? He's an a-hole. Moorish as in Moors. The Moors were Arabs who invaded Spain in the Middle Ages. The Spaniards thought that anyone with dark skin was black, even though they were Arabs from North Africa. *I* would have been considered black."

"But I'm not Arab..."

"I know. He was trying to be funny. *Trying*. And failing."

They both laughed. Rafe said, "There are a lot of a-hole teachers here..."

They both stood in front of their respective classrooms, in the little alcove made between the rows of metal lockers. Other boys squeezed in. A black-haired kid with an acne-ridden face shoved past Mahalala roughly, "Outta the way, Mahalala Dingdong."

Rafe grabbed the boy's shoulder, before he entered the classroom. The black-haired boy stopped. His facial expression changed quickly from confusion to outrage.

"Lemme go," he demanded.

Rafe said, "Didn't your mother teach no manners? You say, 'excuse me.' And his name is Mahalala. Or Rahul."

The boy—Rafe vaguely recalled he was Michael Something-Or-Other—squirmed out of his grip. "Jeez, okay man. Don't get all gangsta on me."

Rafe laughed. "Gangsta? You call that gangsta? You'll know when I get gangsta on you."

Michael Something-Or-Other backed up and slipped into the classroom. He and Mahalala tracked his progress.

"Thanks, dude," said Rahul. He looked at the floor, as if he were ashamed.

"No prob. Catch you later."

❖

He was in bed, exhausted, by 9 pm. Rafe didn't remember being so tired when he got home from seventh grade. There was just so much to take in. It wasn't just the school work, though that was hard enough. He had to read pages of history, study Latin grammar, figure out weird mathematical symbols—basically fill his head to bursting. He also had to figure out the culture of Our Lady which, in many ways, was harder than the actual school work. Like Toby, for instance. At first, he seemed like a cool guy. But then it turned out that he had his nasty side, too. Then there was his friend, Sideshow. He hated to admit this, but there were things that Tomás did that were embarrassing—cussing too loudly or saying inappropriate things—like it was the Street. Rafe saw the other boys looking at both of them when Sideshow had one of his outbursts. He and Rafe were sharing earbuds, listening to a new tune, and Sideshow got lost in the music, swaying, dancing and rapping along—"My bitch ain't no Lady Marmalade/My bitch is drunk on haterade"—and Rafe had to quiet him *again*, for about the millionth time. The boys in the hallway paused, all looking at them as if they could smell the stench of the Street wafting off of them. Their fathers—and, frequently, their mothers—were lawyers, doctors, had positions in government, or were CEOs. Rafe? A homeless ex-con and a lunch lady. The other kids probably went home to waterfront condos or those mini-mansions with marble lions on the lawn. They probably imagined that Rafe and Tomás went home to roach-infested hovels with parents who smoked rock. Tomás was one problem, yes. But the other black kids in school—mostly upper classmen—all seemed to come from similar backgrounds as the white kids.

Tomás called them Huxtables. As in, "Look at the Huxtable over there. I bet he likes Maroon 5." The other students ignored Rafe and Tomás as much as anyone did. Unless he was imagining it. It was so damned hard to make friends with people. At Garvey, it had been easy.

❖

Rafe lay in his bed and sighed. This time, he ignored the lilac angel and faced the mask above his bed. The warm, dark energy it exuded was somehow more comforting to him than the delicate white energy of the angel. It reminded him of Pops. He closed his eyes, and the image of the mask floated up behind his closed eyes.

Rafe woke up holding onto the scraps of dreams. He was somewhere in Middle Earth, he was pretty sure.The forest he'd been in was so thick and lush—the sunlight filtered through the green leaves. The branches of the trees were thick enough to hold entire houses. The doors alone were as ornate as any church engraving. Rafe crouched on one of the branches, watching the progress of a group of orcs on the ground. They were short, squat, warty creatures, with dull, rotted raisins for eyes. He could hear their perverted tongue—clicks and glottal stops—drifting up to where he was hidden. He discerned that they intended to attack and destroy the ethereal home of the elves and befoul it with their presence. Each orc was misshapen in some unique way. This one had a sad-looking horn protruding from his head. That one had a huge yellow fang that still had meat gristle on it.

We can take them, said Legolas. He'd appeared out of nowhere, stealthy as a cat. He notched an arrow on his silver bow. Rafael did the same with his bow. And the arrows flew, swift and true, into the hearts, eyes, and vital organs of the smelly monsters. Black blood flowed, and some orcs futilely tossed crude spears that missed Rafe and Legolas by a mile. They screeched and died dramatic, gore-flecked deaths, crashing into the ferns and shrubs below.

One orc, presumably the head of the squadron, shrieked in an orcish tongue, which Rafe, in his dream, could understand. “Fie! Let us flee! They are too many and we are ill-prepared.” And the rest of the company fled, waddling away in a pell-mell fashion. Rafe and Legolas laughed as the last of the orcs made their clumsy escape.

“We made a great team—just the two of us!” Rafe said.

“Indeed, we did,” replied Legolas, who was suddenly Toby Nelson. “Let’s celebrate.”

And instead of harps and drums and angelic choirs of elf maidens with garlands of flowers in their hair, Toby-Legolas closed his eyes and leaned in toward Rafe’s face. Toby’s clothes had melted away, and he glistened as if he’d just stepped from the shower—

Rafe woke up at the moment. He clawed toward wakefulness. The dream faded, and when it did, he had the sudden and urgent need to pee. When he flung his blanket off, he found that the front of his PJs were cold and moist. *Had he wet the bed?* Rafe cursed silently in the dark. He pulled off his PJs and found that they were sticky.

It wasn’t pee.

Shame flooded him. Rafe threw on a clean pair of underwear, opened the door to his bedroom. It creaked, as he knew it would. He quickly tiptoed to the bathroom and pissed away the rest of the dream. He thought, *I can throw my PJs at the bottom of the wash. Or I can do the laundry myself.* The only problem was that his mother would think it was strange and might figure out why he was doing laundry. Knowing nothing about the subject, he wondered if detergent was strong enough to erase the stain. But worrying about the particulars of laundry was a stalling tactic. He knew that. Sooner or later, he'd have to face the fact that he was having wet dreams about boys. *White boys.*

CHAPTER SIX
STRANGERS

Rafael knew that something was up by Thursday of that week.

He shared fourth-period algebra with the kid who'd challenged Rahul in the hall. His name with Michael Mercanti, and he and Toby hung out now. It turned out that they'd both gone to St. Agnes, Our Lady of the Woods's feeder elementary school. Mercanti's father did the 6 pm news, and his mother was a judge in family court. Apparently, this made him Somebody, because his parents were Important. Mahalala, his only friend besides Sideshow, had told him this information, as if it were a warning of some kind. Rafe didn't really care. Anyway, Mercanti would give him a wide berth whenever he saw Rafe walking down the hall. In class, Michael would move to the opposite of wherever Rafe sat. It was kind of funny, at first. Rafe had never been a badass. In fact, at Garvey and at the Mercury Towers apartment complex, he was considered a mama's boy, the kind who the church ladies cooed over and called an Upstanding Young Gentleman. So it was nice, for a change, even if the reason for this miscasting was for totally BS reasons. Rafe considered making Mercanti flinch, but thought better of it. The only time he did make Mercanti flinch was when he overheard Mercanti and another boy teasing Seeley with sea lion barking noises.

"Cut it out," Rafe told him. And they stopped immediately, with Mercanti pulling the other boy close and walking away in a clipped manner. Seeley didn't thank him; he seemed to have a "whatever" attitude about being teased.

Then, it became annoying. It started with the whispering. It was obvious that Mercanti was telling his friends something about Rafe. In homeroom, Bradley Freeman, one of Mercanti's friends, would stare at him, then glance away quickly whenever Rafe caught him staring. *What was up with that?* Rafe could almost swear that it was fear, as if he—terminally short, not-Lebron Rafe—could really do some damage. Rafe resolved to ignore it.

At lunch time, Rafe, Sideshow, and Mahalala always sat together, sequestered from the rest of the eighth graders, who had all joined various cliques. It was clear that Rafe was stuck with these two. Not that he cared too much; it just would have been nice to make more friends. It was weird, being Outsiders. Rafe had never been one before. At Garvey, he'd been quite popular. He had no real desire to be super popular, but this—status—it sucked.

One time, at recess, he overheard Mercanti talking to a group of boys that included Toby Nelson. Tomás had been out that day, and Mahalala was busy with another nerdy friend of his, so Rafe was alone. The four boys sat on the front steps. Rafe was on a bench off to the side, reading a book, or trying to. Apparently, he was unseen from this vantage point. He wasn't trying to eavesdrop—it just happened that he could overhear their conversation.

"You're such a pussy, Mercanti," said one of the boys—it sounded like Jonathan Lewis. Lewis's voice cracked every now and then, like kindling. "That kid couldn't take you on. He's what, 5'4" at most? And skinny like a beanpole."

"You didn't hear him," replied Mercanti quietly. "Mom deals with scum like him all the time, sends them to juvie."

Someone laughed. Actually, it was a snort. "Come *on*," said Toby. "That kid's about as gangsta as President Obama."

"Toby," Mercanti said, "you know where he's from? The Hood. Even if he's not violent, he knows people who are."

"You think he knows people who can get some weed?" Toby asked. This lightened the mood—they all laughed. And Rafe thought, *I do know where to get weed.* Everyone knew that Geraldine Brown in apartment 4A sold it to make ends meet. He entertained the idea of bringing Toby some weed, just to get closer to him, but...

No homo.

"I've been down there," said someone else, a kid he didn't recognize. "It's not so rough."

"You're shitting me, Olivetti. What's a lily-white ass cracka like you doing down in niggah-ville?" asked Toby.

All the boys went *shhh* at once.

"What?" asked Toby.

Lewis's voice cracked: "You can't say the N word."

Toby chuckled, "I didn't say 'nigg-er'; I said 'niggah.' And besides, fuck all that PC shit. *They* can say it—why can't we?"

No one answered him. The bell rang. Rafe waited a moment, and let the group of boys go in the building before he did.

❖

"I don't care. They can suck my Dominican dick," said Sideshow a couple of days later, when they were waiting for the bus home. Rafe had told him about how they were being shunned.

Rafe laughed, but he thought, *I wish I didn't care.*

Sideshow continued: "I'm not here to make friends. I'm here to get a goddamned education."

"You sound like one of those reality TV show people, the asshole villains. But really. It's not fair that they think we're some kind of thugs. I mean, I'm not gonna lie. That pisses me off."

A bus, the wrong bus, rattled on by, full of people all crushed up against one another. It spat out cindery exhaust from the tail pipe, and the boys momentarily choked on the diesel fumes.

"Welcome to the real world, son," replied Tomás. Tomás continued: "I don't know why you want to hang around with them, anyway. They're faggots, each and every one of them. In these clothes, *we* look like fags, too."

Rafe didn't look at Sideshow. He didn't say anything in return. He just looked out at the street, with its trees, the leaves changing color, from green to reddish brown. He thought, *Does he know? Can he tell?* Rafe had been very careful. He didn't linger in the showers and only looked into the hollow space in his gym locker as he changed clothes. He didn't like dancing or Lady Gaga, and he was as competitive as anyone. He even made sure to say things about girls and pussy when the subject came up. But he was afraid of slipping, that someone would notice what a fake he was. Everyone was telepathic, as far as Rafe was concerned. A couple of weeks ago, he'd snuck down to the laundry room to wash his stiffened underwear. He could swear that the Latina ladies doing their laundry, speaking in Spanish with knowing looks. *He thinks he's slick.* It had felt like getting away with murder, when the clothes were dry and safely hidden in his book bag.

It seemed like a million years had passed. But Rafe still had to say it—even quietly. "I don't think we look like fags."

"Huh?" said Sideshow.

"I said, I don't think—"

The screeching bus pulling up in front of them interrupted him. The bus was crowded—standing room only. He and Tomás were separated by the crush of people. There was a guy strapped into the wheelchair spot and two women with carts full of groceries. A trio of babies whined. Conversations in at least three different languages filled with cramped space with ambient chatter. And the bus stank: diesel, rubber, sweat, and cheap perfume. The bus passed Our Lady of the Woods. Rafe saw students, some of them his classmates, being picked up in cars of all colors. He caught a glimpse of Toby getting into a candy-red BMW that was driven by a blonde lady with perfect hair in an expensive suit. He hoped that Toby didn't see him on the bus.

White Elephant Mall was busy, for once. Rafe's father thought it was because a new fast-food restaurant that specialized in chicken and biscuits had opened up in the food court.

"You know us and greasy chicken," he said with a laugh. *Us* meant black people, of course. Rafe tried the chicken and couldn't see what the fuss was over. The chicken practically *gleamed* with the grease that made it soggy, and the biscuits were tough little hockey pucks. Rafe ended up throwing his portion away. He saw Pops wince when he did that. Then he rememberedPops buying food for someone other than himself was probably a big deal. He probably could've eaten the rest of Rafe's meal. Rafe toyed with saying, "I'm sorry," but Pops didn't want him to know that he lived in a van. Rafe let the moment pass.

"How's school?" his father asked as they ambled back toward the kiosk.

"Hard work. I have so much homework sometimes that I don't even feel like playing Nintendo afterward."

"That's good—it teaches you discipline. You'll be ready when you get to college."

College. Rafe hadn't even thought about that—it was so far away. Images of old red brick buildings covered in ivy, computer labs with pristine new Apples, and libraries filled scholarly tomes flashed in his head. He'd never been to a college campus—he'd only seen them on TV. The dorm rooms on those shows were filled with blonde-haired co-eds and frat brothers from impossibly rich backgrounds. An occasional Huxtable would show up.

"...about friends?"

"Huh?" said Rafe.

"Have you made any friends?"

"Yes," he replied, tentatively. Sideshow counted as a friend. He wasn't a new friend, exactly. They hadn't been especially close at Garvey, but now they were. And Rahul Mahalala was a kind of friend. He'd even called Rafe one weekend and invited him to a movie on Sunday. Rafe had had to decline–the Mahalalas lived way out in the 'burbs, and it wasn't feasible to take a bus there.

They'd reached the kiosk by this time. Q was standing in front of the rows of masks, yelling at a young man in a 'do rag with a wispy moustache and a Tupac T-shirt. Q's hair was spiky and dyed bubblegum pink.

'Do Rag said, "Mind your own fucking business, faggot."

Rafe's father jogged over to the scene, with Rafe behind. "What's going on?" Pops asked.

Q said, "This guy was trying to steal from you–"

'Do Rag sized up Pops. Rafe could see the glitter of malice in his dull brown eyes. Swiftly, he shoved Q against the kiosk and swiped a handful of black soap and ran. The cart toppled. A zoo of carved wooden animals fell and scattered. A stack of the soap towers fell, along with a bunch of bottles of shea butter lotion. Some of the black rectangles of soap fell and cracked against the floor. Shea butter lotion spilled out in a thick, viscous pool. Pops took after the thief. By this time, a gawking crowd had gathered.

Rafe saw Q groaning on the ground. He went over to him. "You okay?"

"I think so," Q managed. Rafe helped him sit up.

The crowd around them chattered and fiddled with their cell phones. Doubtlessly, some of them were taking pictures and videos that would end up on YouTube or Facebook. An elderly security guard with a grizzle of gray hair in his beard ambled up to the scene. He instructed the crowd to stand back, and spoke to Rafe and Q, who by this time were on one of the mall benches.

Q said, "This dude was hanging around Sam's kiosk, picking through the soap, hair picks, and lotion. I said, 'Hey! The kiosk is closed. They'll be back in minute.' The dude looked like a deer caught in headlights. When he saw me walking over, he said, 'What you gonna do?' And he walked right up to me, like he was gonna punch me or something. That's when I saw Sam and his son here coming up the escalator."

The security officer took down the information on a notepad and then spoke into a walkie-talkie that sputtered with voices blanketed in static. He told them that the police would be around to take a more formal complaint.

Q stood up—apparently he hadn't been hurt, only stunned—and began taking pictures of the damage to the kiosk with his Android. Rafe's father came back a minute later. Rafe jumped up from the bench. Then he stood still. He didn't recognize the man standing and surveying the scene. He looked like Pops, but the expression and the stance were different. His eyes were moist and his face flickered between anger and despair. Q held him back. Pops walked around the overturned cart and took in the landscape of ruined wares. Giraffes with broken necks, elephants missing ears and tusks. Boulders of black soap. Pools of shea butter, knocked over masks. It was the scene of a battle. A battle that had been lost. Rafe's father bent down, putting his face in his hands. He heaved, as if sobbing. And then, the violence that sparked off him emerged. He cursed—obscenities cracked in the air like thunder. Pops kicked the cart and stomped on the broken animals.

Rafe shivered. He'd only seen his father like this during the one visit to jail, two years earlier. It had been bright that day, the sky cloudless and deep blue, with the sun almost platinum bright. Rafe and his mother had taken a taxi from the terminus of the subway station. It was a silent, twenty-minute drive into—well, it wasn't exactly suburbia. There were no houses. And it wasn't really the country—no cows. It was like a ruined landscape. But modern ruins. No pillars or statues with time-smoothed faces and broken arms. There were a couple of warehouses with faded paint and dusty, broken windows. Rafe saw pigeons, like dirty rags flung against the buildings, fluttering in and out of the broken windows. He could barely make out the name of whatever company had once thrived there. A railroad track, rusted and overgrown, abruptly ended. They passed a junkyard full of old cars, twisted into weird shapes, and the cogs of machinery. The junkyard was guarded by two pit bulls, both rain-gray, with nightmare teeth and lolling tongues. Both barked their hate as the cab went by. Finally, Rafe and his mother rolled up in front of the prison.

Ursele paid the taxi driver and told him to come back in two hours. Did the cabbie sneer in judgment of them? Rafe wasn't sure, but he didn't like the look that the cabbie gave them. It was disdain, as if he and his mother were the scum of the earth. This was one visit Rafe would never tell anyone about, ever.

The prison was an unexpectedly bright yellow color—the color of lemons and sunshine. There were six L-shaped lemon-yellow buildings in total, all two stories high. No prison tower loomed over them, there was no armed guard. Rafe found himself sort of disappointed—it wasn't hardcore at all. It was almost cheery. If it weren't behind a heavy-duty fence crowned with coils of barbed wire, it might be mistaken for some kind of recreation center.

A young officer with pockmarked skin led them through security—which mostly consisted of Rafe's mother giving up her purse and cell phone. They were both lightly frisked, then led into the cafeteria, which looked like any school cafeteria. Motivational posters that featured eagles, bears, and mountain lions hung on the walls. The air smelled of old cabbage and disinfectant. Guards were stationed all around, each pose like a plastic army soldier. Rafe noted the guns, clubs, and cans of pepper spray that hung on their belts. All of the guards were expressionless.

An announcement about the visiting hours and various protocols was made over the speaker system, the voice distorted and harsh. The group of prisoners walked in a few minutes later. They walked in single file like a class on a field trip. Orange jump suits with block codes stenciled on them separated them from the visitors and the guards. A white boy a little younger than Rafe was cried, "Daddy!" with wild glee, and burst from the arms of a woman with stringy hair and a beaky nose. He flew toward a man with a shaved head, a Fu Manchu mustache, and a freshly busted lip. A black woman with long wavy hair sauntered up from the group of prisoners. Breasts strained against the orange jumpsuit. Rafe saw the stubble along her jawline, and was confused. Was she a she or a he? She walked up to a hulking visitor in a shiny track suit and planted a big kiss on his face. Other groups of people got together and sat at tables.

At last, Rafe saw his father, at the end of the line. He looked thinner than Rafe had ever seen him, with sunken eyes and hollow cheeks. A patchy beard sprouted on his face, along with angry red razor bumps. He gave Rafe and Ursele a hooded glance and ambled over toward them.

"Rafael," said his mother, "go and hug your father hello. He'd like that." She gave Rafe a slight push.

Rafe made tentatively steps toward this thin stranger. When he reached him, the stranger bent down and gathered Rafe in his embrace. And the stranger became Pops again. There was a certain scent—a clean scentthat Rafe recognized. Beneath the hideous orange clothes were the bones and muscles he'd felt in similar embraces. Pops held him tight. He could hear bones cracking, and Pops saying his name over and over. That hug, those words imparted a strength into Rafe, and suddenly this awful lemon-yellow jail in the middle of an industrial wasteland was bearable.

When they were finished, they walked over to the table where Rafe's mother was. She clutched the edge of the table nervously.

"Sam," she said. And there was so much in that simple utterance: fear, anger, and even a little wisp of hope.

Rafe's father nodded. "Ursele." He said her name like a curse.

She flinched. Just for a moment, then she straightened herself out. "Please sit down. You know that I didn't have to come here. My mother thought it was a bad idea. But I said to her, Rafael needs to see his father, no matter what."

He sat down and pointedly ignored her. He asked Rafe about school and the new place they'd moved to. Rafe asked him about the strange woman or man sitting a few tables over. Wasn't this a men's prison?

Dad laughed, "Oh, that's Patrice. That's a man. But he wants to become a woman."

"But how can you do that?"

His mother interrupted. "I don't think that's appropriate to talk to a child about." Pops turned to her, glowering. Held his gaze.

"The boy is twelve years old. Given what he's been through, I think he's old enough to learn the facts of life." His father turned to him, and said, "Patrice takes hormones—chemicals—that help him—"

"Stop. Stop right now. How dare you. *How dare you.* I told you—" Rafe's mother sputtered. "You want to teach him the facts of life? How about this fact: his daddy is in jail because he refused—for years—to help him out financially." She sat back triumphantly.

Rafe's father simmered with anger. That was the only way he could explain it. His skin, his eyes, his nostrils quivered with energy. Rafe felt tension build. And the Stranger replaced his father again. The

Stranger wore his shape, but it wasn't Pops. The Stranger was a being of pure anger. Rafe's father said, quietly, "I'm in jail because you put me here. You knew damn well that I couldn't afford child support. You didn't do it out of need. You did it out of spite. Because you're an evil woman, Ursele. Behind all that Jesus talk lies a heart made of stone."

Rafe's mother opened her mouth, and Rafe could almost see the words about fly from her mouth. They were barbed and jagged, words of glass. She closed her mouth, and turned the words into a gesture. She slapped Rafe's father across the mouth. It was a loud sound that echoed in the fake-cheery cafeteria. Everyone stopped their conversations and stared at them.

Rafe watched his father's hands ball into fists. Rafe knew that his father would kill his mother if he could. He put his hand on Pops's forearm. He could feel the resistance in each muscle.

A prison guard, as square-jawed and blank-faced as G.I. Joe, materialized next to them.

"Is anything the matter?" the guard asked. It wasn't a question, though—it was a warning. Rafe noticed the guard's hand hovering above his belt, ready to seize any one of the weapons that hung there.

The Stranger retreated. Muscles relaxed. But Pops still glared at Rafe's mother. "I think," Pops said slowly, "that this visit is over." He stood up and walked away from them. Rafe could feel the suppressed violence in the air. It was like static electricity. He saw the other families flinch when his father passed them.

The Stranger had been unleashed, again, in the

mall. The Stranger crushed things and then abruptly left, as if the anger that fueled him was gone. What was left was Pops—as broken as the objects around him. The rampage was over. He sat down on bench, and buried his face in his hands. His whole body shook.

Rafe realized that Q had released him, but he was hesitant to go to his father. What if the Stranger returned? That worried him, as did seeing his father defeated. It made Rafe not exactly nauseous, but there was a stone in his stomach—it felt like he'd been kicked there. He tentatively put an arm around father.

Pops was in his own world of sorrow and didn't seem to notice.

"It'll be okay," Rafe said. He felt like a phony. He was just a kid—what could he do? But he kept on saying soothing words.

The new angel was an opaque, milky blue and stood next to its lilac sibling. Both were faceless and in the same pose. They faced the Dan mask: two against one. Rafe's mother wasn't home when he got back from the scene at the mall. On the bus ride home, he resolved to tell his mother about his father's problems—all of them. It was the only thing he could think of doing. He knew his mother wasn't in a good position either, but she was certainly better off than Pops.

Rafe had stuck around while his father talked to the police and cringed when the officer asked if he had any insurance on the ruined goods. Rafe and his father spent the rest of the time fixing up the kiosk and salvaging what they could. Rafe hoped that once his mother heard the story, she would help out. But the new angel suddenly appearing on his desk was creepy. He couldn't quite put his finger on it.

Rafe's mother came home half an hour later, carrying a basket of clean laundry. He could smell the warm spring scent of the dryer sheet.

"Help me put this away," she said.

He took a clump of clothes to fold on the kitchen table.

"How was your father?" she asked, working on her own pile on the sofa, in front of the TV.

Rafe paused. If he told her about the kiosk, what reaction would she have? She hated his father. The nastiness at the prison flashed in his mind. But recently, she'd been really getting into church. When she felt well, she would go to Imani Faith, to one of their evening events. And she talked about angels all the time. She heard their glass voices everywhere. She didn't see them anymore, like the time she'd told Rafe about a few weeks ago. But she said she heard the angel voices every now and then. At first, Rafe sort of ignored it. For instance, his mother would say, "She told me today would be a good day," or "He didn't want me going out in this weather." It was like his mother was daring him to ask, "Who?" even though he knew who "she" or "he" was. Having his mother come right out and say "the angel" would have been a step too far, would be another problem he'd have to face. And he wasn't ready for that, not yet. Anyway, since his mother was all into this God stuff, and God was all about love and forgiveness, Rafe would tell her about Dad.

Rafe took a breath. "Pops is not so good. A thug

tried to steal some stuff from his kiosk, but we caught him in the act. So he destroyed the stuff, instead."

"What?" Rafe's Mom dropped a pair of socks. "Are you—is he—okay?" She looked genuinely worried, her eyes wide, her hands playing nervously in the air, steepling and unsteepling.

Rafe told her the story, but he left out his father's insane, Hulk-like burst of rage at the end. And honestly, he didn't want to think about it.

That close to his father, Rafe could smell the sour stink that was masked by the chemical smell of pink sink soap. Gray strands curled at the roots of Pops' dreads. After Pops shivered and shook for what seemed like ages, Rafe pulled away from him and left him there. He and Q cleaned up the kiosk, throwing away the broken animals and damaged soap. Luckily, none of the masks were damaged. Rafe and Q locked them safely away. Q suggested that Pops go home after the police had taken down his statement.

Pops's face was hidden when Q told him this. When he lifted his face out of his hands, the face was worse than the face of the Stranger. Anger, Rafe could understand. The look on his father's face wasn't anger. It was the face of a broken man, someone whose soul has been pissed on, and who had to accept it. His father's glare didn't even see him. He looked right through Rafe, as if he were a ghost. It was a blank expression that got inside of him, so that he felt the same burned-out, empty feeling that his father felt. It was the look you gave when you saw a dying cockroach, legs wriggling in the air, or a pigeon corpse shellacked to the pavement. Buildings with a thousand broken windows that didn't bother to glitter, they were so full of grime. He'd seen that look on homeless people, their teeth rotted out. It was a look that did not—*could not*—acknowledge that there was any beauty in the world. Rafe left his father there—it was time to get the bus home. He didn't even say goodbye.

After Rafe finished, they sat in silence for a few moments. Rafe went back to folding clothes. He stared at the fabric of shirt until it became all warp and weft. The suspense was killing him.

Finally, he said, "Well?" He didn't look at her.

"I don't know what to say. I mean, I'm sorry that Sam—your father—had to deal with that."

That was a good start, Rafe thought. *Sympathy was better than contempt.*

"But," she continued, "that's what happens when you turn away from the Lord."

For the second time that day, Rafael felt like he'd been punched in the gut. He turned to her, so angry he almost couldn't breathe. He found some words —*you're an evil woman, Ursele, behind all that Jesus talk lies a heart of stone*— and discarded them. He said, "Why do you say that? Why can't you just be nice?" He knew he sounded like a petulant child. He couldn't help it.

"Oh, baby," she said. "I don't mean to hurt your feelings. But you've got to know. *She* told me that your father has surrounded him himself with—well, with *darkness*."

Rafe heard the emphasis in the words "she" and "darkness." The words curled with hidden meaning. "She" was the angel—the glass-voiced lilac one. The invisible voice that spoke to her. Rafe had tried to convince himself that it was harmless, that it was a religion-fueled fantasy that helped his mother through a hard time. Something that made her feel better, like Rafe's fantasy novels or Ninetendo DS games. But now, he wasn't so sure. He didn't want to know, but had to know.

"Surrounded himself with darkness," he said. He watched her carefully. Every blink, fidget, and breath. And yes, it was there. That feverish look in her eyes.

"Yes, baby. Can't you feel it? It comes from those masks he sells. She told me they are evil. Sometimes, I can hear that thing above your bed talking—whispering."

"So... those angels—thanks for the new one—they stand against the whispering mask..." Rafe said this slowly. It was absurd, what she was saying. Like the plot of a straight-to-DVD horror film with lots of blurred shots, cheap CGI, and terrible acting. Rafe thought that she'd laugh at any minute.

But she... smiled. "Yes! I know you love that thing, but *she* told me that—"

Suddenly, it was too much. A wave of fatigue broke over Rafe. His face, his fingers, even his bones all felt like they weighed hundreds of pounds. His eyes burned. The apartment they lived in was small—so small. Too small. The walls loomed and closed in, cement predators. The radiator-heated air was too hot, too dry; he felt like he was in the goddamned desert. The ceiling closed in on him. Every crack and bump threatened to burst like bruised skin, raining pus, paint chips, and asbestos down on him.

"I have to leave," Rafe said to his mother. Or whoever this angel-obsessed woman was. If his father became the Stranger, who did his mother become? It didn't matter. He wasn't even sure that he'd spoken aloud. He just had to get out. Even the carpet clawed at him.

The hall, with its broken lights, worn welcome mats, and cold linoleum stretched before him endlessly, before the doors to the elevator. Outside, it was raining, misting really. Rafe didn't care. It was soothing, if a little cold. And if tears spilled down his face, they would be camouflaged by the weather. He took a breath, then another one. He willed himself not to think about anything. Instead, Rafe focused on the moisture-blurred landscape. The playground that rose out of a wood chipped area, with a swing set and rusted jungle gym. The group of teenagers in another building's doorway, smoking and shooting the shit. The police car with its blue and red lights on, silently sliding up the street. But the thoughts came anyway, as persistent as gnats. They flew through his mind, in a cloud. *Dad is homeless and barely hanging onto his sanity. And Mom has lost her sanity—she's certifiably whacked.*

If home was ever a sanctuary, it sure wasn't now.

Rafe stayed outside until it got too dark and too cold. When he stepped back inside, he brought both the dark and cold with him. Numbness was the only solution.

Behind the Mask

The forest is just beyond the empty playground, where it looms dark and ominous, like a fairy-tale wood that harbors witches, ogres, and Gollum. Rafe must go to the forest, first of all, because he's dreaming. And second, because he ain't no pussy. No homo. He walks past the school, now a ruin with broken windows, strangled by dead ivy and infested with stone gargoyles that leer at him and stick out their tongues. He gives the gargoyles, which are sometimes alive, the finger. In one window, the Lady peers out, white and virginal and eyeless, and he immediately feels shame. But that doesn't last long—there's an adventure to have and those woods aren't gonna come to him. Except they do, in the strange geography of dreams. Walking to the woods is a blur, landmarks flying fast and furious by him. Isn't that the swing set that's in the apartment complex playground? And that jungle gym—from Garvey Elementary. Past Our Lady of the Woods's soccer field. It's all mashed up together like the worst rap song ever, the kind with a million ideas at once, samples, singing, old-school scratches, and some uncool person guesting, like Justin Bieber or Katy Perry.

Anyway, Rafe goes past the jigsaw-like,

Freddy Krueger dreamscape and comes to the Brothers Grimm wood. It's not so scary. In fact, it's kinda nice. In real life, the trees are bare sticks, the ground muddy and covered with decayed leaves and candy wrappers. Here, the leaves are the gold and russet colors that Rafe's always reading about in those English novels, and the trees are tall and reach to the sky, not like the ghetto-ass shrubs that he passes by. The clouds have parted and the sky is that particular blue that he remembers when he and his mother would play hooky from work and school and go to the zoo or maybe a walk in the park. Rafe walks in the woods, lost and not caring one bit. It looked ominous, seen from that broken-down school, but once you were in it, it was wonderful.

So Rafe walks in the wood for a while, not thinking a thing about his mother and her whispering glass angels, or his father and his broke-down van filled with merchandise from who-knows-where. He leaves them behind, along with Toby, Angus, and Sideshow.

But this is a dream—they always change or warp and mutate. And this one does, suddenly, like a jarringly off-key note or a frozen video game. It resets.

It's the trees. They have faces. No, not exactly faces, but masks. All kinds of masks. There are those cheap supermarket Halloween masks that vaguely look like Batman or Superman. Some trees have more ornate masks, ones with jewels and feathers in shapes like the crescent moon or butterflies. Some masks are like the ones his father sells at the mall. The masks don't hang from strings—they just grow out of the wood. He walks past hundreds of the tree-

masks, until Rafe comes to one—The Mask—and it pops out of the tree. Rafe reaches out and catches it.

Rafe knows its significance. It's sacred—made from the wood of the oldest tree, decorated with shells from the sea and the bones of totemic animals. The mask chose him.

Rafe puts the mask on. It glides on and forms a seal around his face. It feels like his own skin. It's as if nerve endings have broken through and fused with the wood, the bones, the shells. The straw is his hair—the tufts that were left on the barber's floor, regrown. His face is fearsome, but also beautiful, so that it doesn't matter how small he is. A glare from the face will stop douchebags dead in their tracks.

Rafe runs through the forest, scaring creatures he comes across, like deer, raccoons, and other half-seen woodland creatures. They don't see Rafe—they see tusks and teeth. And Rafe realizes that he must never take the mask off, because then, everyone would see how weak he was.

And what would happen then?

CHAPTER SEVEN
(No) Homo Erectus

"I smell like a hog," Toby said as the rest of the class entered the locker room. Everyone was drenched in sweat. Loomis had had them run laps in the gym in preparation for some fitness test. It was grueling. Rafe had had to walk for a couple of laps at the end. Every nerve and tendon ached, and breathing felt like inhaling fire. Only the most athletic had been able to run the entire time, and even they lagged at the very end of the exercise.

"Come on, ladies," Loomis had shouted. "One more lap. I know you can do it."

Harrison, a slim, dark-haired boy with a lazy eye, had groaned at that bit of encouragement. Loomis noticed, and said, "Do I need to get smelling salts for Miss Harrison?" Most of the other boys were too tired to laugh at that quip.

Jesus Christ, that man is an asshole, Rafe thought.

Rafe wished that he *was* the thug they thought he was at that moment. Wouldn't it be cool to see Loomis loose his shit? But it would never happen. Rafe, like everyone else, endured the abuse. Who was there to tell, anyway? Maybe this is what Our Lady of the Woods was going to be like for the next five years—kids who ignored you and asshole teachers. Sideshow called Loomis "Loony" once to his face. He'd gotten in trouble, and sent home with a note.

"Alls I said was, 'Sure enough, Mr. Loony,' and he flips his lid. Musta hit too close to home. I guess people called that cross-eyed faggot 'Loony' when he was a kid."

At this point, Rafe could walk in a shower and not notice the other boys. For the most part, the teasing had let up. Seeley the Sea Lion's aloofness had paid offpeople just ignored him, even loony Loomis. This time, Rafe looked forward to the shower. Even tepid water with sudden jolts of freezing jets was better than the sticky, stinky feeling on his skin. He was unused to the way the hair underneath his arms and at his crotch held dark, musky smells. But at least he wasn't alone—water and soap freely flowed over tired and aching bodies and carried pungent scents down the central drains. For once, everyone was silent as they let the water soothe their muscles. Rafe almost felt normal. No one could see behind his mask.

So of course, his mask slipped.

The thing was, Rafe wasn't looking anywhere—just at the beige tile, really—and he got a peripheral glance at Toby, muscular, lithe, rose and gold, the shape of his buttocks, the gentle swell. Not even a full glance, and he felt the butterflies stirring and before he knew it, his dick tingled. He didn't even have to look at it to know that it betrayed him.

Legolas, in dew. Rafe jerked his head away quickly. Maybe it was time for another exorcism by pink soap. But it was much too late for that.

"He has an effin' chubby," someone said. *Freeman? Lewis?* It didn't matter.

Rafe ignored grunts, the lone "ewww," the

cackles, and focused on finishing up. *Why wouldn't his dick stop swelling?* He turned off the warm water and let the shock of the cold water do its work. There was still some cross-talk, though, that made it through his feigned indifference.

"It's not that big. I thought they all had monster dongs..."

"It's disgusting." "Who was he looking at?" "I think he was looking at Nelson."

If this had been a bad movie, those words would be put on heavy reverb. Rafe turned off the shower and wrapped himself in a towel without drying himself. He walked out of the maze, but not before he heard, "Hey, Nelson, you have a boyfriend" in tones that dripped with venom.

Rafe quickly dried himself off. He didn't do such a good job—his back was still damp, so he had trouble putting his undershirt on. It didn't matter. He had to get out of there as quickly as possible.

Please. Please let me get out of here.

Rafe prayed to his mother's invisible angels, to his father's masks. To God. To the Lady of the Woods.

None of them listened to him. *Why would they?*

He had his pants on when he heard Toby, towel wrapped around his lower half, his torso starred with droplets, say to him, "Were you checking me out?" Even angry, Toby looked angelic. And, dammit, Rafe's dick still stirred in spite of everything.

"No, man. I don't know what you're talking about." Rafe held Toby's gaze.

"I'll fucking kill you if you did. I swear. I don't care how *hood* you think you are."

The tension-filled moment lasted forever. Neither

of them moved. Then someone laughed, breaking the spell. Rafe turned from Toby and quickly put on the rest of his clothes.

❖

Maybe they won't say anything.

❖

Latin class went by slowly, in endless drones and declensions. Rafe barely paid attention. Luckily, no one paid him any mind. It was a lecture day, and Mr. Dubois loved the sound of his own voice, so he didn't notice that several students had mentally checked out. The lecture had something to do with how Latin informed scientific language. When Rafe wasn't studying the blue lines on his graph paper, certain scenes played in his head.

You know that short black kid, Rafael? He got a hard-on in the shower after gym.

"Homo erectus," blathered Dubois, "is a term used by biologists, for instance, to describe that humankind..."

You know why he got a stiffy? Cause he was drooling over Nelson.

Homo erectus, Rafe wrote on the graph tablet. He crossed it out. Then he wrote it again, this time in block letters. Then he wrote a big "No" in front of the phrase:

No Homo Erectus.

Then he crossed the phrase out entirely. He blackened it with ink, until it hid behind a thicket of cross-hatched lines, impossible to penetrate.

But *No Homo Erectus* had made an impression

on the pad of paper, a couple of sheets deep. The phrase taunted him invisibly from the squares of blue. The blue lines were the same color as Toby's eyes.

During math class, as equations flowed across blackboards and computer screens, Seeley the Sea Lion stared at him. His mouth was open in that annoying way that made him look like a retard. He sucked air like he was a fish on dry land. He did nothing to hide the fact that he was staring at Rafe. *What was he thinking?* It was impossible to read him.

Was he thinking, *Poor Rafe, they shouldn't have picked on him.*

Or, *I may be fat, but at least I'm not a fag*. Or even, *He's kind of cute.*

All the possibilities made Rafe's skin crawl. With Seeley's eyes on him, he couldn't space out. It kept the dread close to the surface. Seeley had been a witness. He had seen it all. He might have even been the one to call him out—Rafe had no idea of what Seeley's voice sounded like. To Rafe, he was just a pair of eyes in a marshmallow face. He wished that Seeley would stop staring, even if he meant well.

Rafe silently willed the large boy to leave him alone. He tried to focus on the numbers and shapes of geometry, but he couldn't. The trapezoids fell apart. The triangles were lopsided. His pencil wasn't sharp enough and the instructor, Mr. Powell, had a monotone. And boring through it all, like the eye of Sauron, was Seeley's gaze.

Rafe planned to avoid lunch all together. It wasn't like he was hungry—in fact, he felt quite nauseated. His stomach had an entire sea inside, full of dead butterflies. The salty-sour mixture churned, and Rafe felt beads of sweat, each bead exquisitely itchy, form on his forehead. Maybe he could claim illness and go home. Except no one could pick him up. His mother was either at work or talking to angels. And his father—Pops was a lost cause. His kiosk—Chiwara—was on the verge of being closed.

Sideshow saw Rafe in the hall. "Mahalala said he was bringing his mother's chocolate-chip cookies to share." *Rahul—had he seen what had happened in gym class?*

Who the hell cared about cookies? Couldn't Tomás see that he was ill? Apparently not. Sideshow nattered on, oblivious.

Rafe managed, "I'll see you there in a sec," and ducked into the boy's room.

If Our Shady Lady was sleek and outfitted with the latest tech—iPads, computer labs—the bathrooms were a throwback. It was like all boy's rooms everywhere. Tile the color and texture of overcooked roast beef. Grimeencrusted grout. The stalls were the color of gray putty, and the ceiling had a constellation of bubblegum and maybe boogers. The room smelled like pee and urinal cakes. Under normal circumstances, Rafe would have been disgusted. But he was desperate. So, he rushed into an empty stall. The bowl of the toilet had stuff floating in it, a soup of bright orange-yellow with mudballs—Rafe spewed forth, adding to the mix.

What came out was white and thick, the color of buttermilk. Things came up, tickling his throat, falling into the toilet bowl. *The wings of all those dead butterflies?* In between spasms, images flashed of golden Legolas, with his gold-tipped arrows. Then his father's face, slowly becoming the Stranger's, when he learned what he had as a son. Then the sneers and snarls of the boys in that locker room, which surely was in a dimension adjacent to hell.

When Rafe's stomach had nothing else to offer, he briefly laid his hot head against the cool but filthy porcelain base of the toilet, which doubtlessly teemed with a thousand bacteria and diseases. After that, Rafe flushed the toxic stew. At the sink, as he splashed water on his face, he saw, in the mirror, that Olivetti was looking at him. *Had he been there the entire time?* There was no way of telling. Just as there was no way of knowing whether the disgust on Olivetti's face was due to his present bout of puking or the rumors Rafe now imagined.

He heard Toby-Legolas's voice again: *I'll fucking kill you.*

And it was disgust written on Olivetti's face, the scrunched lip, the wrinkled nostrils. That, and contempt. He was no longer afraid of Rafe, apparently. Rafe had changed from Scary Thug to Gross Black Boy.

When Olivetti left the bathroom, Rafe was alone. He looked at himself in the mirror. The scratched and cloudy mirror-image stared back. *So, I have to assume that they know, already. It's the only way I can survive this.* He nodded to his mirror image, like the corny fool he was, and turned to the bathroom door.

Mahalala and Sideshow were sitting in their usual place, away from everyone. Rafe ignored the rest of the lunch room and went over to them.

"Where were you?" asked Sideshow. "Lunch is almost over."

"I—I had to go to the bathroom."

"Damn. Dropping your kids off at the pool, huh?"

Both Tomás and Rahul laughed. Rafe only felt nauseated, thinking about the vomit.

Rahul gave no indication of the locker room confrontation. Maybe he'd left before it happened.

A plastic baggie of cookies was slid over to him. The cookies' shape and texture disgusted him—the bumps, the ridges, the flecks of chocolate.

"I'm not hungry," Rafe said. "I feel kinda sick."

At least Mahalala changed his demeanor. "Oh, man. I'm sorry to hear that. You look a little... green."

"Dude, he don't look green. I never seen a black man look *green*," said Sideshow, ever the joker.

And Mahalala was ever the straight man, over-literal. "He doesn't *literally* look green. It's just a saying, fool. Look at his skin—it isn't green, but it's kind of..."

"Ashy," Sideshow supplied. "Yeah!"

Rafe was over it. They could banter all day, as far as he was concerned. His stomach burbled, and the world swung in and out of focus.

A few tables away, Rafe saw Toby and his friends. Olivetti had joined them. What were they talking about? Rafe both wanted and didn't want to know. He wanted to hide, to bury himself in his closet-bedroom, beneath his covers after drinking a bottle of Nyquil. He also wanted to end the suspense that weighed on him. He saw himself getting up from the table, heading toward Toby, and throwing something—maybe milk—on him, challenging him. He would be the thug that everyone expected himto be. *Better that than a faggot.* But he was too cowardly for that. *After all, he was a faggot.*

Rahul and Tomás chattered on and on. Rafe barely heard them. He watched Toby hold court. He saw the back of his head. Olivetti sat facing Toby and, therefore, Rafe. Rafe tried to look away, to ignore the boys' conversation, but he just couldn't.

I should go. I should go. Rafe chanted it to himself.

The second before he was about to excuse himself, he saw it start. The unravelling of his life. Olivetti locked eyes with Rafe, across the room, as Toby spoke with much gesticulation. Olivetti's eyes widened. He started laughing and pointed at Rafe. Toby's head spun around.

Rafe stood up so quickly that both Mahalala and Sideshow were startled.

"What the f—" started out of Sideshow's mouth.

At that moment, like some divine intervention was it his mother's angels? —the bell rang. Rafe felt its electronic clang vibrate through him. At once, hundreds of boys in burgundy and grey stood as one. A potential crisis was averted.

As Rafe let himself be pulled away by the crowd, he knew that this reprieve was brief.

❖

He rode the bus home alone. It was a good thing

that Tomás had somewhere else to be. Even if Sideshow hadn't heard the rumors by now, his constant chatter wasn't what Rafe needed. He needed to be alone with his thoughts. Rafe didn't really think as he rode through the approaching dusk. He just sat and watched the changing vista, from affluence to run-down. Watched the winter sun fall behind the buildings, and blue and gray seep across the streets. He didn't turn on his off-brand MP3 player that held only 75 songs or crack open the book he was currently reading—the first *Game of Thrones* novel. He enjoyed *not* thinking, for once.

Rafe was so lost in un-thought that he almost missed his stop. It was fully dark by the time he got off the bus, thanks to Daylight Savings Time. Not that it matteredred and blue police lights were ricocheting off the apartment walls when he got home. Someone from the complex, a woman with red braids woven into her hair, was hysterically sobbing out some story while two white officers calmly took down the information.

A thought wormed its way into Rafe's brain.

I hate this place.

Violence was as common as rain—a storm of men hitting girlfriends, mothers hitting children, endless screaming and cussing. The police visited daily. From his window, especially in high summer, he heard all manner of fights, verbal and otherwise. It was never clean. Beer bottles, rose-shaped crack pipes, candy wrappers, Arizona Iced Tea cans, cigarette butts... they were in the laundry room, in neglected corners, everywhere in the playground. Once, he found a used condom near the rusting swing set. It looked like a slug after it had been been doused with salt. Sometimes, older, grizzled men would sleep in doorways or on benches. Afterward, the area where they slept always smelled of pee.

What was Toby's life like? Rafe wondered. He probably lived in a house with a lawn as clean as Astroturf. He probably had his own room, with a large bed and a desktop computer that he owned, not one rented from the school. Rafe imagined an army of servants with leafblowers and maid uniforms, keeping everything tidy. Maybe a purebred dog or two frolicking on the TV-perfect lawn. Now, Rafe would never know.

Rafe moved past the drama, into his own apartment tower, and took the elevator. Fresh graffiti, this time in English, was scrawled on the back wall, a swell of vile words his mother would have punished him for if he had ever said them.

When Rafe opened the apartment door, he knew that something was wrong, even before he crossed the threshold. His skin tingled, and the term *dark energy* came his mind.

The door to his bedroom was ajar, light spilling from the crack. He heard his mother mumbling in there. Rafe stood still, trying to catch the words, which came out in a rush, in a strange flood.

"Where did you go? Did I offend you? Is it something that I did? Please, speak me to again, let me know that what I can do to get your voice back, your voice is sacred and beautiful and soothing and you wrap me up in your love, the love of the Father, the blessings of the Virgin. Please let me know how to help my family, my beautiful son. I would do anything to hear you again..."

His mother was praying. Endlessly praying to her invisible voice. But something was wrong. That sick feeling that Rafe had puked out returned—the dead butterflies in his gut were reanimated. Zombie butterflies—zombieflies. He had to stop this, now.

"Mom?" he called.

She stopped her litany immediately and opened the door to his room, as if nothing had happened. An anxious thought entered his mind: maybe she'd been "triggered" by finding pair of his stiffened underwear, evidence of his sin. Shame flooded Rafe. He'd been mostly meticulous in hiding away his soiled clothes, But his mother's face revealed nothing. She just smiled and kissed him, as if her behavior a minute earlier was perfectly normal.

Rafe told her that he had to get started on some homework, that he'd be out for dinner.

Rafe quickly closed the door to his room. He flipped on the laptop, entered his password, and extracted a textbook from his book bag. But he couldn't focus on any of it, not the screen or the text book. It all blurred. He took a deep breath.

I'll fucking kill you.

Rafe wiped whatever was in his eyes away. He stretched his neck, cracked his knuckles. It was time to bury himself in homework. But something caught his eye, before he turned back to the computer screen.

The new angel was clear, like frozen water. Its wings flared outward, as if it had just alighted on his desk. This glass angel was different than the others, less whimsical. Though it didn't have a proper face, Rafe felt the sculpture had an aggressive look to it.

Plus, it looked expensivecould Rafe's mother really afford it?

I'm not going to think about that.

There were just too many thoughts and emotions invading his head right now. Rafe closed the laptop and the textbook and went to lie down—he'd do his homework after dinner. But there was one more surprise waiting for him.

The Dan mask above his bed, the one his father had given him, was gone.but lately he'd slacked off.

CHAPTER EIGHT
MARKS

The bus had to turn just one corner, and Our Lady of the Woods would be in view. If Rafe rang the bell now, he could get off the bus and skip school. *Where would he go?* It didn't matter. He toyed with the idea of going out to White Elephant Mall and telling his father about his problem. Surely Pops would know what to do. But Rafe nixed that idea—he hadn't really spoken to his father after the incident at the kiosk. The cheap cell phone his father used told Rafe "This mobile customer could not be reached at the moment" in a robo-voice. That blank, mechanical voice never meant anything good. What if Rafe got to the mall and found Chiwara empty? *No.* He couldn't handle that. Not knowing about his father's current situation was a good thing. Maybe he could just bum around downtown during school hours. Hang around comic book shops and game arcades. But he looked even younger than his fourteen years. He'd probably be caught, and then the school would call his mother at work.

Rafe sighed. It was better to just to face the music. He was already an outcast because he was black and poor. Maybe he could get used to a couple of months of being *the Faggot.*

Just as Rafe had that thought, the bus turned the

corner and made the decision for him. There was no backing out now.

When Rafe got off the bus, he noticed a couple of police cars parked in front of the school and three police officers on the wide steps leading up to the entrance. The vice principal, Mr. Bowding, was deep in discussion with them. A fourth officer prowled around the side of the school, in front of a section of the beige brick that was marked with a green smear of graffiti. The officer took pictures, and a couple of students pulled out their smart phones and did the same. Rafe momentarily forgot about his problems with Toby and headed toward the graffiti.

"It's just nonsense," one of seniors said. His cheeks and chin were covered with little blood-spotted tissues, as if he'd had a disaster shaving that morning.

"Looks like paisley," his friend replied—this kid had a significant overbite.

Idiots, thought Rafe. He could clearly see the word "Mantis" scrawled in highly stylized script. The "M" was a puffy arch that encompassed the elongated, slightly tilting "antis," which was further obscured by little flourishes and marks. Rafe had seen thousands of these tags in his neighborhood. After a while, you could read them. They were the street version of runes or Tolkien's Elvish script. This tag was a metallic green, the color of a dragon's scale.

Tissue-Face said, "You'd think that if you were going to vandalize something, you'd at least have something to say."

Over-Bite replied, "You know *they* can't read, much less spell."

Before he thought better of it, Rafe said, "It says

'Mantis.' There are probably others just like that one."

Both seniors turned and looked at him, as if he'd suddenly materialized out of thin air. They wore twin expressions of incredulity, mouths hanging open like doofuses. It was beautiful. But short-lived.

The police officers and the vice principal broke up the gathering of gawking students and ushered them into the school. All the chatter as he went down the hall was about the graffiti. Rafe heard boys excitedly talking about drug-turf wars, like you saw on *Law & Order* or *The Wire*. Rafe didn't see what the big deal was, or even why the cops were called in the first place. At Garvey, markings like these were common. The side of the school was a palimpsest of tags, drawings, and long-abandoned murals. You just got the janitor to cover up the worst ones with that awful rust-red paint. But that was the difference between Garvey and Our Shady Lady. Red paint would never suffice for the pristine walls of the school. They'd probably have to be repainted. Rafe had a quick, evil thought: he hoped that Mantis would show up again, should the walls be repainted.

In home room, everyone was chattering about the graffiti. Everyone, that was, except Brian Ogilvy. He'd stopped chewing his nails to stare at Rafe. The look vacillated between disgust and amusement, as if he were mesmerized by a spot of dog shit on Rafe's shoe. Ogilvy's eyes glittered with malice. His body language said, *I know your dirty little secret*. It also said, *Faggot*.

Ogilvy looked away from Rafe and started to talking to Theo, who was tossing out wild theories about the Bloods and MS13.

"Chill," Rafe told the owl-faced Theo. "The Bloods are in L.A. This isn't exactly MS13's stomping grounds."

That statement stopped them chattering. Theo said after a pause, "How do you know so much about this stuff?"

"You know where I live?" Rafe replied. That elicited a couple of nervous giggles.

"Yeah, right," said Oglivy. He said it just loud enough to turn some people's heads.

A confused silence settled in the room. Ogilvy was issuing a half-hearted challenge. Everyone could sense the tension in the air. Shame flooded Rafe and was quickly replaced by anger.

"What do you mean, Ogilvy?" Rafe asked through clenched teeth.

Ogilvy held his gaze for a moment, then seemed to think better of it. "Nothing," he said, in a way that clearly said, *this isn't over*.

"Why don't you say what you mean?" Rafe knew he was being reckless, but he was tired of always being timid. *What was the worst that could happen, really?* Ogilvy would accuse him of being a faggot, and Rafe would deny it. He almost relished the opportunity. A kind of bloodlust filled him. He didn't care that Ogilvy was bigger than he was. He didn't care if he got hurt. Maybe—just maybe—word of Rafe whupping Ogilvy's ass would get around and the awful episode in the locker room shower would be erased. It would be worth the pain and the trouble.

"*You* know," Ogilvy said.

The moment was interrupted by Angus O'Connell entering the homeroom. Every boy looked away from the ensuing fight. If O'Connell detected any of the built-up tension, he gave no indication of it. Instead, he announced, "There's going be an assembly in fifteen minutes. Let's go."

This isn't about that damned tag, is it? And yet Rafe knew it was. Everyone stood up and formed a line, as if they were elementary school students. As they filed out into the hall, with O'Connell leading the group, Rafe stepped behind Ogilvy and yanked his blazer.

"What the—" the boy started, but Rafe shushed him.

"What was that about, in there? What were you on about?"

Ogilvy looked annoyed. Then, he grinned. "*You* know," he said. His voice came out in an oily slither. His gums were thick and pinkish brown, *like Pepto Bismol mixed with diarrhea,* Rafe thought.

"If you have something to say, say it." Rafe felt his teeth clench.

Ogilvy rolled his eyes, like a googly-eyed Muppet. "Everybody knows that you were jerking off in the shower, looking at Nelson."

That hit Rafe like a bowling ball to the stomach. Rafe's rage, his desire to beat the pudgy freak to a pulp, ended right then and there. It was worse than he thought. *Not only was he a homo, he was a perv.*

"Who told you that? It's a lie!"

Ogilvy shrugged.

"Who, dammit!" Rafe shoved the boy. By this time, all the students were filing up the hallway to the auditorium. A couple of boys stared at them.

"Don't get your panties in a bunch. It's on Facebook. Don't know whose. I forget." Ogilvy walked away.

Rafe didn't do Facebook. His mother had had a MySpace page for a hot minute, and he'd played on there briefly, but never made the leap to Facebook, mostly because computers and Internet connections were scarce. When they'd finally bought the refurbished offbrand laptop—one or two years out of date—he mostly used it to play games, the bootleg and freeware versions of them, since games were memory hogs. But everyone at Our Lady of the Woods was on Facebook. Now, everyone did everything on Facebook. And that included telling lies.

It was bad enough to have a recounting of his mishap go around school. But now it was floating out in cyberspace, where anyone could see it. Rafe could see it now, a wall posting on Toby's profile: *Did you see that kid pulling his pud in the shower when he looked at you?*

Someone would read that and, by day's end, Rafe would have practically tried to have sex with Toby.

"Rafael Fannen!" The sound of his name brought Rafe back to the here and now of surging upstream to the assembly hall. Angus O'Connell ran through the sea of boys, parted them, and reached Rafe. Rafe had been standing in the middle of the raging sea of boys, like a piece of driftwood. *Let them drown him, let them trample him, kill the queer.*

"Come on," said the chaplain. He looked flustered and slightly ill.

Rafe listlessly moved with him. O'Connell asked, "What was the hold up?"

"Nothing," Rafe mumbled. But in his mind, the comments and "likes" on that Facebook posting just grew and grew. Words and nasty images, some of which lived deep down in his mind. Hadn't he "pulled his pud" at the sight of Toby's nude body—in his dreams? The last wet dream had been a couple of days ago. It hadn't even been in Middle Earth. It was just a blur of contorted body parts and movement. Even now, the zombieflies of shame stirred in his belly. He barely noticed O'Connell guiding him to a seat next to the rest of his home room. Rafe saw Ogilvy chewing his fingernails. He felt sick. Rafe glanced around the auditorium. Whispers bounced off the floor, the ceiling, the cinderblocks. Some of them, surely, were about him.

That scholarship kid's a faggot!

A nigger and *a queer?*

Rafe studied the faces around him. Was that junior staring at him? Why was that kid with the braces looking at him? Every glance, every lip movement was potential treachery. Rafe's skin itched. He could almost see the distortion as if it were a vaporous mist spreading across the school. It flashed on the screens of iPhones and iPads, and slithered from mouth to ear. He heard the words nearly everyday in the apartment halls and buses.

Pansy. Sissy. Cocksucker. Bitchboy.

And those were the nicer ones.

Mr. Bowding stepped up to the microphone on stage. A squall of feedback effectively shushed the crowd but did nothing to calm Rafe's racing mind.

Pipesmoker.

"I'll make this brief," said Bowding. He had a tiny red mouth in a pumpkin-sized face, washed-out blue eyes, and thinning, curly hair. "As I'm sure you all know, Our Lady of the Woods was vandalized last night. It is the police department's opinion that a person outside of our community is responsible. We have called you all here to help monitor our community—make sure that it's safe. Because it is *our* community. If you see any untoward behavior or suspicious activity, please report it to a teacher or administrator immediately."

Bowding droned on for a few more minutes, and a word salad of buzzwords—togetherness, community, zero tolerance—competed with the imagined whispers of the boys seated around Rafe—*Fudgepacker*. The impromptu—and to Rafe, pointless—assembly ended with a brief question-and-answer session.

During this time, Rafe formulated a rudimentary plan. He would avoid gym class today, and possibly lunch as well. It was hardly foolproof, and carried many risks. But the alternative—facing Toby again and the potential savaging of the lunchroom gauntlet—was unbearable, at least for today. Let him build up some resolve, some plausible story about why he had a chubby. *I was thinking about Nicki Minaj*. But where could he hide out?

The statue of Our Lady gazed serenely at Rafe as he read *A Game of Thrones* in an unused, dust-free pew. The lights were off, so filtered stained-glass colors were his reading lights. Our Lady was splashed with ruby, sapphire, and emerald. She wasn't nearly as creepy as his mother's angels, in spite of seeming to float on her carpeted dais. Rafe had felt only a slight twinge of apprehension as he walked away from gym class—he was sure that he'd pass some of his classmates. But he was lucky. No one caught him going the wrong direction. Loomis never took attendance. Rafe's absence might be noticed, but it was possible that it would not be noted. Besides, this was only for one day, while he considered his options.

Sneaking into the chapel was like sneaking into a forgotten temple. It smelled of old incense and cleanliness, wood soap and stone. The glimmering darkness invited him. It was as if no one had been in here for hundreds of years. By closing the doors behind him, Rafe shut out the rest of the modern world. He was in a sacred space.

Rafe put away his book. The sex scene he had been reading seemed wrong in this environment. He should use this time to reflect, anyway. This was just a brief interlude. He'd just stay here until he got himself together.

He found himself on his knees, in front Our Lady. Praying.

He prayed for himself. *Please don't make me a homo. Homos get killed where I come from, shot right in the face and left to rot in back alleys. I know, I heard it in the laundry room about a body they found not two blocks away, and they called it a hate crime. They already hate me. Don't give them another reason to hate me.*

He prayed for his father. *Help him, please. I just want him safe and not living in a dirty van.*

And he prayed for his mother. *Please—make*

those voices go away. Bring back my old mom, Ursele, not this frightened, sick woman.

I'm sorry I called you Our Shady Lady. You're not shady at all. You're bright and glowing. You're my Luminous Lady.

Rafe found himself crying—the emerald, ruby, and sapphire smeared together. He cried silently.

Did Luminous Galadriel listen?

The chapel door opened with a creak. Instinctively, Rafe crouched down, even though he knew it would do no good. The harsh light of the school hallway penetrated the thick, jeweled gloom of the chapel. Immediately, he saw it was the chaplain. O'Connell saw him, too. The chaplain let the door fall close.

"What have we here?" he asked, in that dorky way of his, like he was a comic book arch-villain finding a spy.

Rafe sat up.

The two of them regarded each other for what seemed like a long time before O'Connell broke the silence with, "What are you doing here? Don't you have class?"

Rafe fully intended to tell him something, some convincing lie—*I'm praying* or *class was canceled*—but what came out were words that bypassed his brain and came straight from his soul: "I need help." Rafe's voice even cracked, dammit. O'Connell gave him a welcoming smile, one that mirrored the shape of the Luminous Lady's, and gestured him into the adjoining office.

The office was different from the time Rafe had first been in there. The walls were covered with pencil drawings, men and women in superhero poses. A woman in a skintight outfit with a billowing cape held a kind of wheel fringed with razors. "Catherine" was written beneath her fierce crouch in block letters. Another image showed a man pin-cushioned with arrows—he was in the process of removing an arrow from one of his wounds and notching it in a bow. He was "Sebastian."

Rafe sat down across from O'Connell, who was feverishly writing some kind of note. When he finished after dramatically dotting an I, he looked up. "What's up?"

Rafe paused. *What should I tell him?*

"It's my family," he said. "My dad lost his job, and my mother is getting sicker..."

There was a lurch in his stomach. Just saying those words sounded like a betrayal, an admission of weakness. *Poor nigger child from a broken home.* It was obscene, saying these words to a white man. It was something that a pansy-ass faggot would do. Angus looked at him encouragingly. *Go on,* said the look. But Rafe thought O'Connell was secretly getting off on his misery, like a pervert. *No. This was a bad idea.*

"Never mind," Rafe said and stood up. He didn't know where he would go—just not being *here* was more important than any destination.

"Where are you going?"

Rafe didn't reply. He just walked out of the small office, into the gloom of chapel.

Suddenly, he felt O'Connell's hand on his

shoulder. It didn't restrain him—the touch was too gentle for that. "Don't go," O'Connell said.

Rafe paused. In that pause, it all came down, the wall he was carefully building. He shuddered, shattered. Everything blurred. *Damn, I'm a pussy. A faggot.*

Rafe was enfolded in arms, against black vestments. It all swirled together in his head, a vicious tornado: his mother's angels and weird prayers. His father's broken masks and dirty van. Toby's hate. Rafe's wet dreams. He heard Angus shushing him, soothing him. O'Connell ushered him back into his office. He sat Rafe down on the chair. At that moment, the bell rang. Rafe stood up automatically. O'Connell pushed him gently back into the chair.

"I'll write a note excusing you from class," he said. "Just stay and we'll get this mess sorted out."

Rafe took an offered tissue and wiped his face.

"What's this about your mother getting sicker?"

When Rafe didn't respond, O'Connell said, "Don't worry. Everything is confidential."

"You promise?"

"I promise."

Rafe started, "My mother has become a different person. It's been about a year..."

Years ago, when Rafe was eleven, his mother had been a different person. She'd been spiritual, rather than religious. She'd go to church now and then, but not with any regularity. "God lives everywhere," she'd said. "I can talk to him in church or at Target." She'd had a full time job as a secretary at a law firm, where she'd typed and formatted legal briefs. She was also taking classes at night to become a paralegal. They'd lived in a nicer area—the "English basement" apartment in a row house. Rafe even had his own real bedroom. The house's upstairs cat, named Emperor, would frequently enter their dwelling and sort of became their unofficial, occasional pet. Rafe's mother would pretend that she hated the filthy, sneaky beast, but every now and then he'd catch her stroking the silver tabby's fur. Once a month, Rafe's mother would take off work and call the office at Garvey, telling them Rafe was sick. He and his mother would play hooky. During those days, she would instruct him not to call her Mom, but Ursele, her first name. "Today, we aren't mother and son—we're friends." They might go to the zoo that day and spend hours watching the monkeys mugging for attention. Or they would go to the movies, catching matinees. Or go to a museum exhibit. After that, they would go to lunch, often at one of Rafe's favorite restaurants. It had old, wooden floors and was full of ferns and time-darkened portraits. He'd always order French onion soup, with its cheese-crisped crouton floating over rich beef broth, and Ursele would have sesame chicken salad. The rest of the day they might walk in the park, next to the greenish-brown creek or, if it was raining, go shopping for toys or go to the library. Ursele was the one who turned Rafe onto reading. Though not much of a reader herself, she encouraged Rafe and bought him books, mostly from yard sales or church bazaars. Her hair was in a natural then, and she wore make-up.

He missed those U & R days, as he called them.

Then, it all began to change. The job at the law firm was downsized and they moved when the row house was sold. Ursele took a job as a cashier in a hospital cafeteria and had to delay the paralegal courses. "Damn—I could have been Erin Brockovich!" There were no more U & R days, something Rafe understood at twelve, even if he was disappointed. The new digs were depressing, but until then Ursele had kept a doggedly positive outlook. "It's just temporary, baby, just a brief spot of trouble," she told Rafe.

Rafe could almost remember the exact day she changed. It was a Sunday morning. Ursele woke him up at 6:30 a.m. and told him to get dressed for church. She'd already taken her shower. Rafe was groggy—he'd been up late the night before watching a horror movie on TV and hadn't had enough sleep. But his mother was adamant and, frankly, kind of bitchy about it. They had to go to church, and *don't you give me that look, young man*. Rafe grudgingly dressed in stiff clothes and they were at the bus stop by 7:45, along with a group of church ladies in silly hats. Rafe's mother's hat—she was decidedly no longer Ursele—was wide-brimmed and black. Her outfit was a magenta pencil skirt and jacket, trimmed in black. She wore faux pearl earrings. On the bus, his mother revealed why she'd had the sudden urge to go to church.

"We have to get right with the Lord, Rafael. I think it's time we pay Him the respect He's due."

"But," Rafe said, still sleepy and lulled by the purr of the bus, "you said that God is everywhere."

She paused, this new version of his mother, and replied, "I was wrong. *They* told me I was wrong."

He hadn't really been paying attention and was still kind of pissed at her. Even so, the mention of *they* mildly disturbed his carefully maintained ignorance. *Who were they?* Some supernatural instinct or intuition stopped him from asking.

Rafe and his mother sat through the service, with its sermons and spirituals. Rafe was mostly bored, opting to look at the stained-glass windows, which had all of the saints and angels depicted as black folk. Squares of bright color splashed on hats, shirts, and pews. The service wasn't that long—it ended an hour later. As the last acolyte ambled down the aisle and folks headed for the refectory, Rafe's mother stayed behind. When they were last people in the fellowship hall, she began to walk around the empty room, frantically, as if she were looking for something. She walked up the dais, where Jesus hung rather peacefully on a cross behind sprays of lilies. She shook her head, if not at the Savior, then something in her mind. She left the dais, examined the font, and found just ordinary holy water in the cistern. Then she went to each window and studied the figures there. Moses was found lacking, as were Jonah and his whale.

"What are you looking for?" Rafe asked.

His mother didn't even turn from her search. She said, "Don't worry, baby. I'm sure I'll find it. Why don't you go down and get something to eat? I'll be down in a moment."

Rafe left her there, and went down the stairs to where people were talking and laughing. Silver pots of coffee steamed, and pink punch made of some frozen block of pink ice and 7-UP fizzled. Everyone seemed to know everyone else, so Rafe got a Dixie cup of punch, which tasted like liquid candy, and some stale supermarket cookies, found an empty chair, and sat down. He seemed to sit there forever. Sometimes, a lady or a man would nod in the benevolent, noncommittal way that strangers do. Rafe counted the passing moments by trips he made to get more punch—it was better when the pink stuff was diluted with more soda. When folks started leaving, Rafe stood up and decided to look for his mother.

Rafe tried to ignore his creeping dread as he went back to the fellowship hall. He wasn't sure what he'd find—he couldn't imagine it. *Ursele* was strong and fierce and fearless. Rafe didn't know this strange, fidgety woman who took her place. He was both disturbed and annoyed to find that she wasn't there. Where could she have gotten to?

Rafe wandered the huge church for a good ten minutes, looking for his mother. Into a darkened chapel and the silent kitchen. He was about to go the church office—perhaps there was some sort of intercom system. At this point, he was angry and frightened, though he wouldn't admit that. He finally found her in the lobby, standing in front of the gift shop.

His first thought was, *Thank God, I've found you. Can we go now?*

But his second though was, *What's wrong with her?*

The gift shop was closed, but Rafe's mother was glued against the glass, like a little girl looking at a cute puppy in a pet store. What was she staring at so intently? He sidled up beside her and looked into the dark store. He saw a lighted curio cabinet, full of porcelain and glass figurines.

"They told me it would be there," said his mother. She sounded full of excitement.

Rafe asked her, "What do you mean?"

"See that angel—the one made of crystal?" He did. It was beautiful, prismatic. "I saw it in my dream last night. Except it wasn't really a dream. It was more of a—vision."

She turned to him, tears glittering in her eyes. "Everything is going to be all right. It's all going to be good again." She held his face in her hands. Her gaze was intense, piercing; yet for all that, she didn't seem to *see* him. "I just know good things are coming. The angel of light—that's who I saw—and she looks just like that! That"s why I had to come to church, you see." Her voice was so girlish that she sounded like the white girls at Garvey Elementary squealing over Justin Bieber. "You know, I named you after an angel. Raphael, the angel of healing."

They left Imani shortly afterward. On the bus ride home, Rafe's mother seemed to fidget and squirm, as if she couldn't contain herself. Rafe was torn. It was weird, and he caught some fellow passengers casting sideways glances at her. But she seemed excited. It was the first time in a long while that he'd seen her expressing anything approaching happiness. He wanted his mother to be happy—just not like this.

For the next couple of months, they went to church on Sundays. Rafe eventually made church-only friends and even went to Sunday school. He found he could ignore or downplay the more ostentatious behavior his mother displayed, for the most part, because she was so happy. Like when she sometimes stayed up late, praying in her bedroom. Or when she'd burst spontaneously into song. Or when he heard her talking to herself—or someone. During this time, she would tell him about her dreams or stories about angels, which she developed a keen interest in. They had weird names, like characters in a fantasy game—Uriel and Remiel. Once, he called her an "angel geek." She seemed to like that, and Ursele, or part of her, emerged. But then things got so strange that he *couldn't* ignore them.

Once, he overheard some kids in Sunday school talking about "the angel lady."

"She told my mother that she saw an angel and how it spoke to her in a language that sounded like crystal bells."

"Isn't she the lady who's always singing? She's so happy. *Too* happy, if you ask me."

Another time, Rafe's mother told him that her boss at the cafeteria job had told her to stop talking about seeing and hearing angels.

"The nerve of him," she said over dinner. She'd been agitated throughout the whole meal, dropping food and scraping her plate with the tines of her fork. "All I was doing was telling Sula about a book I was reading about guardian angels. And Willie comes up to me and says that we can't talk about religion at work. But I wasn't talking about religion—I was talking about angels."

Rafe almost pointed out to her that angels were religious, but the way she was acting—fluttering arms, twiddling fingers, shaking voice—stopped him from doing so. She was quivering with a strange energy.

And then she began talking about energy—light energy and dark energy. Angels, of course, were light energy. Anyone she didn't like—Rafe's father, her boss, the woman who shortchanged her at the supermarket, the teenagers who loitered in their building's hallwayswere full of dark energy. Dark energy was everywhere. The air you breathed, the lessons he learned in school. The rats and cockroaches were animated by it. Drug addicts pushed dark energy into their veins. Dark energy powered the world. Only angels, those "luminous beings," could counteract the tide of dark energy that threatened to consume her and her child.

Rafe's mother began to be less happy. Not exactly angry—just easily irritated. She devoted herself to the study of light energy and angels. The crappy laptop they had was full of downloaded papers and images of Seraphim and other orders of angels. Her bedroom was full of books about angels, with titles like *Talking to Your Guardian Angel* and *Angel Magic*. These books were heavily marked up, underlined, with circled words, as if Rafe's mother was studying for some divine exam.

One day, Rafe came home from school and found his mother lying on the couch, asleep. There was something about the way she was lying—her arms crossed over her chest as if she were a corpse—and the slack expression on her face made him try to shake her awake. Her eyes slowly opened, as if she'd been deeply asleep. It seemed as if her soul was taking it's time settling back into her body.

"Hey, baby," she said. Her breath was slightly sour. Rafe could smell coffee.

"Mom, are you all right?"

"No, baby. I'm ill."

"Oh no! What's wrong?"

"I couldn't go into work today. I just felt exhausted.

I could hardly get out of bed this morning. Even pushing the numbers on the phone made me ache, deep in my finger bones. I'm just so tired. If I could just get some more sleep, I'm sure I'll be all right."

Rafe's mother gave him a weak smile and slipped back to sleep. Rafe stayed up that night, keep vigil over her. *Should he call the hospital?* He ended up calling his father, who just told him to keep an eye on her for a day. Neither of Rafe's parents had insurance, and medical bills were expensive without it. Thankfully, the next day was a Saturday, so Rafe didn't have to skip school. It was noon the next day when Rafe's mother emerged from slumber. Rafe hounded her to go the doctor—there was a free clinic in the northeast quadrant of town. He called a taxi, and they waited for an hour before the doctor could see them. The doctor took some blood from her, noted her symptoms—lethargy, wandering aches—and gave her Tylenol. Rafe's mother slept through Sunday, skipping church. By the afternoon, she could shuffle around a little bit and managed to make a salad to accompany the pizza they'd ordered.

Rafe's mother managed to get to work on Monday, just barely. By Wednesday, the results of the tests came in. *Inconclusive.*

"I think," his mother said one night, several days later, "I've been infected by dark energy. *They* no longer speak to me."

Rafe sat back after telling O'Connell most of his story. In spite of his apprehension, Rafe felt better. This was something he couldn't tell anyone, not even himself. Now that he'd told someone—an authority figure—maybe, just maybe, someone would tell him what to do.

O'Connell sat back, steepling his fingers. "Huh," he said. And that "huh" was a kick in Rafe's gut. Rafe could see the wheels spinning in O'Connell's head. Phrases like *Disadvantaged Youth* and *Poor Nigger Child* must be shuffling through his mind. Rafe looked away from him. *What could this white man, probably from some hoitytoity university, do to help him?*

"I'm glad you told me," the chaplain said, finally. "It sounds like... I don't want to get ahead of myself, here, but it sounds like your mom.... Listen, Rafe, do you know what bipolar disorder or manic depression means?"

Something filled Rafe's stomach, something thick and wriggling. The zombieflies churned in his belly. Rafe was going to puke, he was sure of it.

"Yeah. It means that Mom is crazy."

"No, it doesn't mean that at all."

Images of straight jackets, padded cells, and Hannibal Lechter swirled in Rafe's mind. *No, no, no.* There was no way—how could he deal with—what was he going to do?

"Rafael Fannen, listen to me." O'Connell stood up and walked over to him. "It just means that her brain is wired differently. There might be a chemical imbalance. It does *not* mean that she's crazy."

"But—the voices. The angels." The crystal angels that looked down at him in his room took on a sinister meaning.

"With the right medication, she can get better. The voices and the hallucinations will get under control."

"Medication—you mean stuff like Prozac?"

O'Connell nodded. "Something like that. She just has to see a doctor."

"A... psych doctor."

Rafe had seen horror movies where cruel doctors in crisp lab coats strapped women down and shoved gleaming needles into their arms, or placed crowns of metal connected by spider-web wires to machines on patients' heads and zapped them with electricity. The convulsing faces, the bodies shuddering with seizure. How could he make his mother do that?

"Would you like me to talk to her?"

Another image flashed in Rafe's mind. Behind the strange mood shifts, the ever-present fear, the illness, the angel wings, was Ursele still there?

"I don't know," Rafe replied honestly. He'd have to think on it. He had a deep, visceral reaction to anyone, let alone someone from his school, speaking to his mother. But maybe she'd listen to O'Connell, because he was a man of God.

The bell rang. Two hours—gym and lunch—had passed. It was time to go.

"I'm here if and when you need me," said O'Connell, when Rafe stood up. Rafe extended his hand. O'Connell ignored it and enveloped him in an embrace.

Black fabric scratched his cheek, the scent of some weird soap filled his nostrils, and he felt the thumpthump-thump of O'Connell's heart. Hands caressed Rafe's skull. Rafe resisted, and O'Connell held him a second or two longer, as if he didn't want him to escape.

When he was finally released, Rafe walked away

quickly, out of the office, past the Luminous Lady, into the stream of students in the hall.

Maybe I imagined it. It could have been anything. But what could it have been? No, I imagined it.

When Rafe had been pressed tightly against the chaplain, his stomach had been adjacent to O'Connell's crotch. Through the fabric, Rafe swore he'd felt something in O'Connell's pants. It could have been anything, like a pen, Rafe thought. *Yes, a pen, that was it. A pen.*

CHAPTER NINE
HOMONYMS

The next morning, Rafe found himself in Mordor. It wasn't a land of craggy rocks and lava rivers and steaming volcanoes. No giant spiders lurked in caves. But orcs were there, all the same. They just wore uniforms. Toby and his friends took on the role of the ringwraiths. Toby was their natural leader, the Witch-King—he was no longer Legolas. His handsomeness had evaporated. Rafe now saw him as a bony, pale, too-thin creature. His ice-blue eyes reminded Rafe of the blue discs of concentrated cleanser you put in toilet bowls. His blond hair was thin, and he had no ass. In spite of that, Toby still lurked in Rafe's dreams. No more soft explosions at night. No, just nightmares and moments spent waiting for the next encounter.

They wasted no time.

Rafe spun the dial of his combination lock and heard a group of boys, with Toby in the center, talking about him. They whispered among themselves, as if they were afraid him, as if he were some kind of wild animal. *No sudden movements, or the homo will spit out venom.*

Rafe messed up the lock's combination a couple of times—ignoring the boys was hard work. When he finally got his locker open, Toby seemed ready to pounce.

"Hey, *Gayfe*," he said, "we missed you in gym class yesterday."

Snickers, shuffling shoes, barely suppressed giggles. It was like a TV laugh track.

Rafe turned around and faced Toby. He didn't say anything.

Olivetti said, "He's giving you a look. The Look of Love."

Chuckles and chortles that detonated like machinegun fire.

"Ooo, baby, I want you in me," said Freeman. He closed his eyes and panted in mock ecstasy.

Everyone laughed at the performance. Rafe grabbed his books and pushed through the semicircle of boys blocking him. As he left the mob, someone grabbed the back of his shirt collar, hard. Then Rafe was pushed, and he crashed right into a locker. Rafe's cheek grazed the edge of a combination lock.

In homeroom, a group of students stopped talking amongst themselves when Rafe entered. He walked past them and went to his seat. Their dead eyes followed him, tracking him, as if he were some unpredictable monster. Disgust was the main expression, the more show-offy version of it, followed by amusement and, in one case, pity from the boy with the owl glasses. Rafe could only imagine what they were saying. Things like this tended to get out of hand. Once, at Garvey, a boy in his class, DeVaughn, had sprained his ankle over the weekend, playing kickball. By lunchtime, it had become a broken foot while chasing some hoods. Rafe knew that cell phones and Facebook pages were probably full of lies and exaggerations. He'd made a point not to look at the computer when he got back home last night. Maybe he should have—at least he would have been prepared. But he couldn't. Rafe didn't eat last night—not that his mother noticed, she was mourning the fact that angels didn't speak to her anymore—and he fell asleep around 3 am, watching the shadows with their dark energy dance on his ceiling.

Rafe sat down, pulled a book from his book bag, and tried to read it. But he felt them leering at him, could almost hear the thoughts that tumbled through their heads. Words he'd heard on the street, on the bus, on the subway. The words of the textbook in front of him blurred. They could have been written in the Black Speech of the orcs—he couldn't read them.

O'Connell stepped into the classroom and everyone settled down. He led them in prayer. Rafe couldn't get into it, so he kept his eyes open. And he saw Noah Crowley seated in the circle across from him holding up a piece of notebook paper that had a drawing on it, done in blue ink. A crude doodle of a boy leered at the crotch of another, taller boy. The ink boy was colored in, crosshatches of blue lines. He had wide saucer eyes and an open O of a mouth as he gazed at a bulge. The look on Noah's face was malevolent—he was quite proud of his drawing and of the horrified look on Rafe's face.

"Amen," finished O'Connell, and the picture was quickly buried beneath a textbook.

A berserker's rage rose from somewhere and made Rafe's face tingle. He ran across the room, pushed Noah down, and stomped on his throat. With his foot still on Noah's throat—which made his pasty face turn as blue as ink—Rafe extracted the paper from his pile of books, and ripped it to shreds. The foul picture fluttered down like snow on the Noah's gasping face.

Except that Rafe didn't. He just sat in his seat, looking at the scowling boy's face, until Noah squirmed and said, "Stop looking at me. I'm not a faggot—I like *girls*."

All ambient chatter stopped. There might have been a gasp from someone.

"Noah Crowley!" said O'Connell. His face was flushed with red anger. "We do not use that language at Our Lady of the Woods!"

"But—" Noah sputtered.

"Not one more word, or you'll get an instant demerit."

Noah looked down at the pile of books on his desk, thoroughly embarrassed by the rebuke. It was a hollow victory, though. Noah still had the drawing and, more importantly, another reason to hate Rafe. Rafe knew this wasn't over. So did the other kids in class. He could tell, because the usual murmur of voices had stopped. The room was thick with tension. It was like humidity—molecules of superheated angst and resentment bumped against each other. The electronic bell ended the silence. Everyone scattered and headed into the hall.

"Rafael," said O'Connell after most of the

boys were out of the classroom. "I'd like to speak to you for a moment."

When they were alone, O'Connell put his hand on Rafe's shoulder. It was an intimate gesture, one Rafe didn't feel comfortable with. It made him feel... *weird.*

"What happened?" O'Connell asked. He stroked Rafe's cheek, touching the spot where Rafe's face had hit the locker during the earlier run-in with Toby and his crew.

"Nothing," said Rafe. "I just slipped on some ice on the way to the bus stop."

They both knew that he was lying. O'Connell tightened his hold on Rafe's shoulder.

"Listen," he said, "you let me know if anyone's bothering you. That's the last thing you need."

Who was he, his official protector?

"I have to tell you something," O'Connell continued. "The vice principal, Mr. Bowding, wants to talk to you."

"Why?"

O'Connell sighed. "I think it has to do with the graffiti. Come, I'll walk you there."

The two of them walked down the rapidly emptying hallway. O'Connell said, "I think that Bowding is investigating the vandalism. I know you didn't have anything to do with it, Rafe. But he just wants to talk to students... randomly." O'Connell said that last word, "randomly," with scare quotes. Apparently, he thought the investigation was BS. Rafe could guess why.

Mrs. Murtaugh, the school secretary, sat at her computer. Her hair was hidden by a colorful scarf, the kind cancer patients wore. Her eyebrows looked drawn on and were crooked. O'Connell left Rafe in the waiting area after giving his shoulder an awkward squeeze. Bowding's office door was flanked by two panels of pebbled glass, the kind that distorted what was behind them. Rafe could make out a large plant blocking the left panel and, on the right one, the blurry shape of a person.

The door swung open and out stepped Tomás. He swaggered out. He said, without looking back, "I am *not* the droid you're looking for, dude."

Rafe couldn't help but laugh. Sideshow was crazy. He certainly had more balls than Rafe had.

Sideshow turned around and saw Rafe sitting there. He stared at him for what seemed to be a long moment, as if he were undecided whether to speak to him or not. That's how Rafe knew he'd heard the rumors about him. He was sized up in that gaze. Words—*pansy, fag, cakeboy*—ping-ponged in Sideshow's brain. Finally, Tomás settled on something neutral: "Good luck with the Inquisition." Then he turned around.

Rafe almost said, "Wait. Let me explain..."

But he didn't have the chance. Mrs. Murtaugh said, in a bored, distant voice, "Rafael Fannen, Mr. Bowding will see you now."

Rafe swallowed, composed himself, and walked into the office. Bowding's desk was enormous, the size of a surgical table. His name plate—GERALD ALOYSIUS BOWDING, JR.—faced Rafe. Rafe saw a pile of files on the desk, a couple of books, pictures of a family. The man himself sat behind a humongous monitor screen, and he was typing something into his computer.

"Have a seat," Bowding said, not looking up from the screen.

Rafe sat in the hard, uncomfortable wooden chair and waited while Bowding finished up whatever he was typing. He turned away from the screen and gave Rafe a huge smile, as insincere and devious as Gollum's. In fact, he kind of looked like Gollum, back when he was still a hobbit named Smeagol. Something about the fleshy face, the dead eyes that sparkled with some unknown agenda. There was a mole on the right side of Bowding's jaw—it was the size and color of a cranberry. His mouth was small and puckered, like a butthole.

"How're ya doing, buddy?" he said.

"Okay, I guess..."

"Right, right. Good." Bowding glanced at the screen. Apparently there was some information about Rafe on there. He wanted to know what it said.

"I bet you're wondering why I asked you to see me. I'll put you out of your suspense. I'm just asking students if they know anything about the, uh, *incident* earlier this week."

The cranberry mole jiggled with each movement of Bowding's mouth. In a way, it was mesmerizing. Bowding paused, as if inviting Rafe to speak. When Rafe didn't respond, he continued. "You know, I'm not just the vice principal of Our Lady of the Woods. I'm an alumnus. Class of '84. I'm very proud of this school. So, if you know anything about this"—a quick glance to the computer screen—"Mantis, I'd—in fact, the whole Our Lady of the Woods community—would greatly appreciate it."

Rafe had nothing to say. *Was he supposed to know this Mantis guy because he was from the inner city?*

Even his mother would know that was some racist BS. He toyed with saying, *Yeah, I know Mantis. Tyrell Wilkerson, down on Baltimore Avenue.*

When Rafe didn't say anything, Bowding spoke again, this time with less smiling. "Lemme reason with you, Rafael. Someone said you knew about this graffiti artist."

"What the" —and Rafe remembered about the two seniors who couldn't decipher the tag. "I didn't say I *knew* him. I told them—those boys—just what the tag said."

Bowding's face furrowed. It was the type of expression an exasperated Gollum would have. Rafe half-expected him to talk about "nasty hobbiteses." The butthole-mouth puckered. "Right," Bowding said. His white skin was slightly flushed. Bowding looked at a stack of some official-looking folders and started to rifle through them, as if he had something important to do. He obviously didn't believe Rafe. "Well, that's all, Mr. Fannen."

He was dismissed. Rafe almost—almost—told him that he honestly didn't know who had painted the school wall. But it wouldn't have been any use.

Rafe was late to class, of course. Mrs. Murtaugh had handed him a hall pass, so at least he had an excuse for being late. For some reason, Mr. Wilkinson, the math instructor, had a bug up his ass when Rafe entered the classroom.

"I see you've decided to join us, Mr. Fannen," he said, pausing in the middle of an equation on the whiteboard.

Rafe mutely handed him the note. It should have shut Mr. Wilkinson up. Instead, Wilkinson sneered at the note and said, “A bit too early in the year for trouble, eh, Mr. Fannen?”

For a moment, Rafe wasn’t sure that he’d heard the teacher right. But he heard the telltale sub-chatter of other students in the room. Then he wanted to punch Mr. Wilkinson, with his black curly neck-beard, right in the throat. But he couldn’t. Of course he couldn’t. He was so angry. Violent images flashed in his brain, like scenes from a horror movie. Smashed fingers, markers shoved up the hairy tunnel of Wilkinson’s nose. The images saturated his mind, his sight, until his eyes filled with tears of frustration. He was so helpless!

Rafe took his seat and pulled out his books. He tried not to notice the force-field of shame around him. He was an outcast. He was a hobbit in a sea of orcs. He forced his anger down deep, until it hardened.

When time for gym class arrived, Rafe found himself walking toward the chapel. There was no way he was going to face that ridicule again. Part of him wished that O’Connell was there. And the other part wished that he wasn’t. On his way down the hall, Rafe passed a group of eighth graders hovering over an iPad. Red-haired Hunter was among them. One of them looked up and said, “That’s him!”

“What?” The word was out of Rafe’s mouth before he knew it.

Hunter silently showed Rafe the screen of the iPad.

There was a grainy picture of him, probably

snapped with a cell phone camera. From the looks of it, it was in a school hallway. The picture had been blown up until the pixels degraded into blurry spots. On the picture's face, someone had crudely drawn what looked like foam dripping from the corners of his mouth. Written above in a childish scrawl were the words "I'M GAYFE AND I LIKE DICK."

If he'd had a gun at the moment, Rafe would have riddled the lot of them with bullets. Then he'd use it on himself. He saw it all go down in front of him—the carnage, the arterial spray, and the sparking, broken iPad falling to the floor.

The boys stared at Rafe. They hadn't figured out the proper response. Hunter's face was unreadable. Rafe walked away from them, quickly, before he could snatch the iPad and smash it or embarrassed himself by crying or screaming with rage. As he moved down the hall, he knew that the image had proliferated and was in a thousand cell phones and computers. It was flying through the air, downloading to a thousand screens.

Rafe reached the sanctuary of the chapel and closed the door. He wasn't alone.

A custodian was busily vacuuming the rug. He had earmuff headphones on and was singing along, quite loudly, to an Usher song. It was so ridiculous that Rafe momentarily forgot about his troubles. If Sideshow had been there, both of them would have fallen out laughing.

Sideshow, who now probably hated him.

It was this thought that brought back the cloud of bleakness. Rafe snuck behind the singing custodian, under the watchful eye of the

Luminous Lady, who hadn't held up her end of their bargain. Rafe slipped inside O'Connell's room. It was empty. *Good.* He could hide out there until lunch period. Rafe noticed that the trashcan and recycling bins where empty, which meant that the custodian already had been in there.

It was dark in O'Connell's office, the only light coming from the window outside. Since the sky was gray and overcast, the room was gloomy. The small alcove reminded him of his own bedroom. It was so small and close. It smelled of disinfectant, and underneath that chemical overlay, there was a churchy smell—musty and full of dry paper. Now that he was alone, Rafe had some time to examine the Saints as Superheroes drawings.

The drawing of St. Thecla showed a woman dressed like a nun fighting off a hoard of wild beasts—scary lions and wolves in some unholy collaboration to take the woman down. The saint was busty, like all women in the comics were, and a weird force-field seemed to protect her. A man wrestled with a lion, aided by a garish yellow halo. Wings sprouted from the back of a boy with a bunch of arrows sticking out of them. O'Connell's drawing skills were good—they weren't cartoony, like many comics Rafe had seen before. Maybe O'Connell had been to art school. He was certainly a geek, much like Rafe himself.

Not knowing what else to do, while he waited until the period was over, Rafe sat down. He knew that he'd get in trouble for skipping gym class twice in a row. And after seeing Bowding, he was already on the radar as a potential problem kid. But after what had happened, what sane person would go back into that lion's den? Rafe couldn't even imagine that his father would blame him.

Pops.

That stung, just the thought of him. Where was he? There was no way he could approach his father with this problem. What father wanted a sissy-faggot for a son? And his mother—she was clearly going off the rails. She'd probably start speaking to angels again, trying to save his soul.

I have no one. I have to do this myself.

He didn't want to think about it. He didn't want to think about anything.

Rafe distracted himself by looking through the papers on O'Connell's desk. There was a chapel service program with a beautifully rendered drawing of the Luminous Lady. Rafe recognized O'Connell's style, his way of crosshatching for shading and, finally, the lettering. He really was a good artist. He had captured the Madonna's gentle mysticism perfectly. Beneath the program was a stack of drawings, mostly sketches of the Virgin. Rafe cycled through them. One was done in charcoal, another, in a light, blue-gray colored pencil.

Rafe moved the blue-gray portrait to reveal the next image beneath.

It wasn't a picture of the Virgin. Or a saint. Or a martyr.

It was a drawing of himself.

The image of Rafe was done in pastels, soft-focus and dewy. Angus O'Connell had captured Rafe in various tones of brown, from warm amber to acorn and chocolate. In this picture, his hair was dreadlocked, like it had been before he'd come to this horror-show of a school. It was a good drawing, maybe even the kind that might hang in a museum. But the Rafe captured in this picture, against the stark white of the paper, was nude. The real Rafe's flesh goose-pimpled when he saw the intimacy of the strokes, those dark circles of his nipples, the genitals that rested in a nest of fuzzy hair.

Something stirred in his stomach, in his bones. He ignored it and carefully put the drawing back underneath the other ones, in the proper order, so O'Connell would never know that the pile had been disturbed. Then he left the office. *Had the door been opened or closed? Closed,* he remembered, *definitely closed, to hide what was on the other side.*

No. Won't think about that.

So Rafe tamped the image of the nude brown boy—*maybe it's not me*—down deep in himself. In the red darkness of the chapel, his eyes fell on the one bright thing there. The Luminous Lady. Her face gazed at his, an eyeless stone glance. But still, she spoke to him, like one of his mother's angels: *Leave,* she said. *Go.*

Rafe obeyed her. So, out of the red, close and sacred, and into the industrial, lonely beige hallway. He didn't think about the paper Rafe. He let the image drift down, to be buried underneath the other things his mind, like a piece of paper lost in his father's messy van. It clouded his every step, that image. It took every bit of concentration *not* to think about it. About the touches and squeezes that O'Connell gave him. The brushes, the gazes.

Rafe found himself at the gym, with no alibi handy for his tardiness. He sat in the bleachers, watching a game of dodge-ball. Loomis didn't even look up from his cell phone screen. Rafe would think of some excuse, if and when the moment came. But Rafe didn't really care. He was beyond caring. Instead, he focused on the echoes in the gym, the squeaking of soles on the gym floor, distant boys' voices. The bleachers slowly filled with boys who had been hit by the red rubber ball.

"Hey, Rafe. So nice of you to show up." It was Toby who broke the spell. He'd just been walloped by the ball and sat in a bleacher a row below Rafe.

"Shut up," Rafe said. It was almost a reflex. That got a chorus of *ooohs*. They sounded like a bunch of pigeons.

Toby beamed with the attention. He actually *smiled.* "I just thought you were being *niggardly.*"

Boy, don't let them call you that! Rafe's father's voice stirred in his mind. Rafe had only been called the N-word playfully, by other black people. It was thrilling, to use a forbidden word, to throw it around. They all knew that white people must never, ever say it. Every boy at Garvey swore a blood oath to beat the ass of any white boy fool enough to utter the word.

He knew that Toby was playing a game of some kind. "Niggardly" wasn't a word that he knew. But the word "nigger" was in that word, hidden in plain sight. An open challenge. Moments after that word emerged, Rafe punched Toby.

He hit Toby in the face. Maybe it would shatter, like a glass angel. The feel of his fist against that face felt so damn satisfying that it flooded his brain. He not only hit Toby—he also hit Legolas. And the nightly dreams. And the whole damn school, from Gerald Aloysius Bowding, Jr. to Angus O'Connell. Rafe raised his hand to hit Toby again and found that he couldn't; someone held him back. Toby, whose head was on his knees, lifted his face. There was a bright red stain on his face. It would bruise up nicely. Toby lunged at him, but someone, another boy, stopped him before he landed a punch. By this time, Loomis had made it over to the bleachers.

Toby ranted and raved. Was that blood glistening on his teeth? He cursed, "That fucker punched me!"

Confusion was the default expression on Loomis's face, so Rafe couldn't really read the gym teacher's expression. Rafe said, "You called me nigger!" It came out as a scream, the ugly slur underlined and followed by a thousand exclamation points.

Toby spat a globule of pink, frothy spit on the gym floor. "You stupid *faggot*. I called you *niggardly*. It's an effing homonym—it just sounds like the N-word. You're just too stupid to know the difference."

Rafe struggled and wrested himself free of whomever had been holding him. He jabbed at Toby—

His jab landed on Loomis's torso.

"That's it. Both of you, stop. Everyone, leave here now. The two of you—come with me. And no more fighting!"

Rafe could feel the hatred rising out of Toby like heat. Rafe felt it, too. He hated everything and everybody. They followed Loomis, standing a hallway width apart. At a turn, when the gym teacher could no longer see them, Toby rushed up and slammed Rafe against a wall.

"Hey!" shouted Loomis. Gasps came from those lingering in the hall. Some said *faggot*. Or *nigger*. Rafe wasn't sure. He just remembered sliding down the wall. Toby had punched him in the stomach, pushing all of the air out. Rafe didn't care what happened—if he got kicked out of Our Lady or not. He just wanted to leave this hellhole.

It seemed like Rafe had been on the bus forever. First, cross-town, then, to the suburbs. Some people looked at him, curious. He must have been a sight, in a rumpled school uniform, with gauze around one hand. *Let them come to their own conclusions.* He checked his hand—the knuckles he'd scraped had stopped bleeding, but they left brownish-red, knuckle-sized smears on the gauze. In spite of it all, he smiled. He'd gotten Toby. That had to count for something. And, more importantly, he'd gotten out of the school. With every mile that the bus went, the more relief he felt.

Rafe had been out of it for most of the time after Toby's attack. Everything was filtered through a strange haze made of adrenalin, hatred, anger, and fear. His entire body just wanted to shut down one moment, lay in stasis like a body in hyperspace, while the next moment he wanted to run. There was also a part of him that wanted to continue the fight with Toby, that wanted it to never end.

Somehow, Rafe had ended up back in Bowding's office. He and Toby sat in seats across from the large desk, with Loomis hovering behind them.

Loomis gave his version of the story, which was garbled, of course. "I don't know what started it, Gerr—Mr. Bowding. They just started fighting each other."

Bowding shook his head, and gave his

best Disappointed-in-You look. "I expected so much more from you, Toby. I mean, both of you."

"He started it," Toby said, full of belligerence. Even in his dazed state, Rafe was surprised at how confident Toby was to interrupt the vice principal.

"He called me the N-word," Rafe said. Both men paused at that.

"I did not." "Yes. You. Did."

"You are so f—. You are so stupid. I called you 'niggardly.' It means lazy."

Both the teacher and the vice principal had confusion frozen on their faces, as if they did not know how to proceed. Rafe swore he saw Bowding's mole change color, from the deep burgundy of the school uniform to a pinkish, Pepto-Bismol shade.

"That's not very nice," Bowding decided on, finally.

"I don't know what the big deal is. *They* call each other that all the time."

That made Rafe want to jump up and punch him again.

"Toby Nelson, enough!" said Bowding. "You know that I'm going to have to notify of your parents. You know we have a zero-tolerance policy about violence in this school. This will go on both of your records."

That seemed to quash Toby's defiance. Rafe guessed that Toby felt the same fear of parental disapproval that he did. Both boys were ushered back into the office area as various numbers were called. They sat across from one another.

Toby shifted from a sullen slouch and whispered, "This isn't over, *Gayfe*. Not by a long shot."

Rafe found that he didn't care. It was actually

kind of funny and pathetic. Toby would hate him, no matter what. Rafe had bigger things to worry about. At most, Toby might get a slap on the wrist from his model parents. The punishment might be no TV for a week or skipping fencing lessons. Rafe actually laughed. Toby was a jerk, like Malfoy in the Harry Potter books, hiding behind his daddy's power.

Toby snarled at him. "What are *you* laughing at?"

Rafe just shook his head. "*You* wouldn't understand. You'll never understand."

Toby didn't have a chance to respond, because Bowding called him into his office. Apparently, they'd reached Toby's mother and she asked to speak to him. Toby's face fell and his demeanor changed upon hearing that. He changed from a vicious asshole into a cowed, sheepish little boy.

Rafe couldn't resist saying, "Give Mommykins my regards."

He wasn't sure Toby had heard him.

The office had been unable to reach Rafe's mother at work, or home, or on her cell, though they'd left messages on each. Rafe had been a little nervous because of that—*where could she have been?* He had them call his father.

Rafe didn't think they'd be able to reach Pops, either. But they did. Whatever phone troubles his father had had were resolved. Rafe waited patiently while Bowding spoke at length to Rafe's father. During that time, Toby was escorted by Mrs. Murtaugh to gather his things at his locker for a half-day suspension. The boy looked positively defeated. Mommykins had probably torn him a new one.

Bowding called Rafe into his office.

"Your father would like to speak to you."

Bowding didn't leave his office, which was intimidating.

"Pops." The word dropped like a stone.

The signal glitched. "Rafe. Can you tell me what happened?" His father's voice was dull, but it might have just been the signal, which faded in and out.

"Yeah. This kid, Toby, has been bothering me since I came here. Real bad. He called me—the N-word. In a weaselly kinda way. In gym class. So..."

He heard the hissing on the other side—static silence.

"I was afraid this would happen," said Pops, finally. "You didn't do the right thing—violence is always wrong. But no one can blame you, either. Where's your mother?"

"Dunno." Rafe turned away from Bowding and whispered in the phone. "I think she's getting worse. I'm worried."

Another pause on the line, the fuzz-silence-fuzz.

Then, "Okay. Let me talk to Mr. Bowding."

Rafe handed the phone back to the vice principal. He overheard his father and Bowding talk for a few minutes, with the vice principal ending with, "I'll send him to you."

When Bowding hung up the phone, he told Rafe that he was to go to his father's place of work. "Under normal circumstances, we have a parent pick up a boy who's been suspended. Have your father call me as soon as you get to his office."

Rafe didn't bother telling Bowding that his father didn't work in an office.

Rafe saw White Elephant Mall in the distance and rang the bell on the bus. He got off a stop early—a brisk walk would help prepare him mentally for whatever mood his father would be in. O'Connell's naked drawing of him drifted into his thoughts, unbidden.

As Rafe left Our Shady Lady, O'Connell had seen Rafe walking out of the building, accompanied by Bowding.

O'Connell intercepted them. "Mr. Bowding," he said, his eyes trained on Rafe, "what's going on here?"

Bowding said, "It seems our Toussaint scholar has gotten himself in a little trouble. Very disappointing, indeed." Rafe ignored Bowding's snarky commentary and studied the young chaplain's face instead. Rafe saw concern in his face. O'Connell gazed at Rafe. That look was like a death ray. It burned away his clothes, seeking what was beneath them. Rafe's brown skin flowed beneath chalk, colored pencil, and whatever material O'Connell had used to recreate his nude body on white paper. Rafe felt feathery fingers gently brushing the finished picture. Fingers that wanted to touch real flesh. And for a moment, just the briefest of moments, Rafe could actually feel those fingers on his skin. He shuddered. Now, he saw that O'Connell, in spite of the things Rafe thought were a little creepy, was as handsome, in his own dorky way, as Toby was. And that thought was terrible. Rafe left the building without a word or a glance back at the two men or that damned school.

Again, Rafe tamped down the nude drawing and its meaning and consigned it the bottom of the drawer of his mind. A light breeze, with a bit of a bite, began to blow as he walked across the mall parking lot. He saw Pops's van. He took a quick minute to glance at it. It looked shiny, and the windows sparkled in the weak light. There was that, at least. He peeked in one of the windows. There was still a mattress in the back, but the interior was clean. There were no more food wrappers or other bits of trash. *What could that mean?* Rafe hoped it was something good.

When he reached Chiwara, he saw that his father actually had a small crowd of maybe six people hovering around the carts. And they weren't interested in just the black soap and shea butter, either. A couple in traditional African garb—the man in a white flowing ensemble with gold-embroidered edges, the woman in a wine-purple gown and matching head-wrap—listened intently as Rafe's father spoke about the history of a mask they were admiring. Rafe's father had also changed. His dreadlocks were gone, replaced by a close-shorn, Barack Obama look. He looked less grungy than he had before. In spite of how awful his day had been, Rafe felt a little bit of joy stirring inside of him.

Rafe caught his father's eye during a lull in the presentation and then went to sit on a bench.

Q came over from Bling My Ring.

"Hey," Rafe said to him. Q's hair was relatively conservative now—it was his natural black and the sides had been shaved off, making a kind of faux-hawk look.

Q nodded in return.

"I bet you're wondering why I'm here, in the middle of a school day."

Q smiled. "Trouble at school? I figured something was up. The Professor kind of told me a little bit. But it's none of my business."

"It's okay."

"Well... I hope you kicked that kid's ass!"

Rafe smiled. It felt good. Maybe Q was all right.

Rafe's father seemed to have made a sale. Rafe saw him wrap up one of the masks in packing paper and place it in a large bag with handles. He beckoned to Rafe.

"Hi, Pops."

His father just hugged him.

After Pops called Bowding to tell him Rafe had arrived, and a couple of more sales, Rafe and his father finally had a chance to talk. Rafe finally told him about the Toby situation.

"What's your mother think of this bullying?" Dad asked, after mulling it over for a few moments.

"She doesn't know. I mean, the last few weeks, she's kind of been in her own little world."

"Well, I think what you did was a necessary evil. I wouldn't recommend it, under any circumstances. But aggression is the only language these bullies understand. When I was... away, there would be a fight in the yard or the common areas. Guards and tasers were no deterrents. Some people just have to *bully*."

"Why me, Pops?"

"You're an intelligent young black man. You're shorter than average. You're a bookworm. Any and all of these are reasons. Which is to say, no reason at all."

Rafe nodded. But it was still an unsatisfying answer. He knew that Toby had somehow seen the real him. And so had O'Connell. Rafe was Gayfe. The mask was slipping.

Pops said that he would drive Rafe home after the kiosk closed. Another stream of customers wandered up to Chiwara, so Rafe left the area and let his father continue to sell. Rafe found himself near Bling My Ring and Q again.

Q looked up from texting and acknowledged him with a nod. "Everything copacetic?"

"I guess." Rafe wanted to *really* talk to Q, but didn't know how.

After a pause, Q said, "It's tough. I know. I left school because of bullying. I wish I hadn't, but, man, it was too much." Q moved from his stool to sit next to Rafe on the bench.

"What—what did they do to you?"

"Oh, everything. Made fun of my background—there were a bunch of guys who'd call me racist names. *Chink. Gook.* Said that my family ate cats. And, of course, fag and queer—or queerboy. I'd get in fights almost every week. Had my locker defaced. Someone put my picture on a gay escort site and I got all these twisted calls. Another time, they wrote my number on a restroom door. Finally, I had had enough. I brought a knife to school and threatened the main bully—a douchebag named Watchell. A good 'ole boy, ha ha! Wouldn't you know it, the little Asian kid gets suspended, while the good 'ole boy gets off smelling like a rose. But it was okay. I mean, it took a couple of years, but I'm doing all right now."

Rafe tried to imagine Q threatening someone with a knife. He was so docile—Rafe couldn't see it. And another thing—the question was on the tip of his tongue. He wanted to ask, *Are you gay?* But he didn't.

"My bully's name is Toby." The words were out of Rafe's mouth before he knew it. "The asshole says that he saw me looking at him in the shower. And told everyone I was gay. He calls me Gayfe. Now it's all over Facebook."

Q winced in sympathy. "Aw, man. You have it rough. This Toby guy really has it out for you."

Rafe said nothing. *What was there to say?* Q hadn't asked if Rafe was gay. Q patted him on the shoulder and said, "You know that you can call me. Or text... one thing that I wish I had had was someone in my corner. You got a cell?"

"Yeah."

"Gimme your digits."

Q programmed Rafe's number with a ringtone that sounded like an arcade game theme—lots of whooshes and blips. "That's so I'll know it's you."

❖

The ride home with Rafe's father was mostly silent. Suburbs—strip malls, Home Depots, office parks, fastfood chains—quickly melted into the warehouses and high-rises of the city outskirts. Rafe learned that his father had fallen off the grid for a little while. Pops claimed that he'd had to move suddenly, due to "a change in the lease," but had finally found a new place.

"It's nothing great—just a room in a group house. But it's something."

His former homelessness wasn't mentioned. Rafe said nothing. His father was too proud. And besides, Rafe told himself, he could have been wrong about that assumption.

Instead, Rafe said, "Business is really picking up for Chiwara."

"It comes in fits and starts," said his father. "But, yeah, it has. Mostly. Quy had an idea, to talk up my place on certain online forums or mention stuff on Craigslist. After that, more people came out. Quy's a smart kid. He really shouldn't be just selling cell phone covers from a mall cart."

"Pops?"

"Yes?"

"Do you think... Is Q gay?"

His father got quiet. They drove through a couple of intersections. Street lights spilled over them in tawny waves.

Finally, Rafe's father said, "I don't know. And I don't care."

CHAPTER TEN
GLASS ANGEL GRENADES

Through the apartment door, Rafe and his father could hear Rafe's mother moving around and mumbling to herself—or to someone. Rafe glanced at his father and saw a worried expression on his face. Rafe felt sick inside. *Dread.* Zombieflies were slipping and sliding in the pit of his stomach. For a moment, Rafe thought that he'd spew right then and there.

"Rafe, open the door," his father said softly. Rafe could tell that his father wanted to be anywhere but here. Rafe obeyed.

The lock took forever to turn, it seemed. When the door opened, it was hard to take in what was before him. Dim light, coming from Rafe's room. Everything covered in soft, gray graininess.

"Ursele!" Rafe's father called out his mother's name.

And like a ghost, she appeared, out of the gray graininess. Rafe saw his mother pacing back and forth on the rug in front of the TV. She wore a beautiful white nightdress with lace piping at the sleeves. Her hair was wrapped up in a scarf. She didn't stop moving. Nor did she acknowledge that her family was standing in the doorway. She just walked on and on in a circular pattern. Something crackled beneath her feet.

"Rafe, turn on the light." His father's voice had an urgency to it.

Rafe flipped the switch. "Ursele!"

Her face was dusted with what looked like sugar crystals, crystals that had left cuts on her cheeks. Cuts that bled bright red. The floor was spangled with small bits of crystal. Rafe saw a glass wing, the color of lilac; a hand, gently tinted amber. Pulverized faces gazed up at him with absurdly peaceful smiles. His mother walked over the crushed angel corpses, barefoot. Slivers, shards, and particles of glass stuck to her feet and they bled, like the soles of a martyr's feet.

"Ursele!" By this time, Rafe's father had reached her. He grabbed her by the shoulders and shook her once. Only then did the faraway look in her eyes fade, only then did she come back from wherever she'd been. Ursele's eyes focused, and recognized his father's face.

"Samuel," she said, finding his name. "They left me. I can't hear them anymore."

Then she crumpled, falling against him.

Rafe and his father had more or less pieced together what has happened from fragments of information by the time the ambulance arrived. Rafe's mother had had what the ambulance attendants called "a psychotic episode." It had started at work, at the hospital cafeteria, when the lack of angelic chatter began to affect her. Ursele had left the cafeteria, claiming illness, and ended up at Imani Faith, where she bought the rest of the glass angel collection.

"But these angels were silent. They had no

voices. They didn't sing to me, like the other ones did," she said. One EMT had given her a sedative by this time. Rafe stood by as the EMTs carefully removed glass from her face and feet and washed them with antiseptic.

"So, I got angry. I know that I should have been patient, but I couldn't wait. So, I... I destroyed them," Rafe's mother said.

Both Rafe and his father listened in quiet horror.

"I wonder if I'll ever hear them again," said his mother. Her voice was thick and slurred as the sedative began to take hold. Rafe curled up next to her on her bed. He took in everything—the smell of her sweat, the antiseptic she'd been treated with, her hairspray. He felt her heart beat slowly.

"Mom, please go with them."

She'd refused to go to the hospital. "I'm not crazy," she said. "I know how they treat folks on the psych ward. 'Naw, baby. I just want to be left alone."

"But Mom, I need you. Even if you never hear them—those angels—again, I will need you."

Tears leaked from Rafe's eyes, but he ignored them. This was too important. It made his problems with Toby and O'Connell seem small and meaningless. Our Shady Lady was nothing compared to this. Maybe—just maybe—the old Ursele would come back, after treatment. But Rafe knew that if *he* had visions of a horror-show psych ward in his mind, his mother must have even more.

"But they'll take them away," his mother said. Her voice was soft and her eyes were closed. "I wish you could hear them."

"Ursele, please," his father chimed in. "You won't

be gone that long. I can take care of Rafael until then."

She opened her eyes this time. It seemed to take a great effort to do so. And she looked straight at Rafe's father. Everyone, including the EMT crew, was silent, waiting for her to say something. It was as if the world had stopped.

"All right," she said. The word dropped like a pin. "I'll go."

There was a collective sigh of relief. Ursele pulled herself out of the bed. She was unsteady, but she made her way to the doorway. She surveyed the landscape of shattered glass in the living room.

"It looks like there was a war up in here," she said, after a moment.

Rafe walked up beside her and took her arm. "It sure does."

She laughed, suddenly, a sound that he hadn't heard from her in months. Her laughter had always been infectious, and he started to laugh as well. He wasn't sure why he laughed. Maybe he just needed the release. Maybe it was only that he enjoyed the feeling, the vibration in the bones, the smile that stretched across his face. It just felt nice. Rafe didn't notice just when his father joined in, nor when the laughter changed, and the three of them were crying.

❖

A light snow drifted over Our Lady of the Woods as Rafe got off the bus. He shivered, and told himself that it was the cold and not any fear about going back to the school. He'd been suspended on a

Wednesday. Though he could have gone back to school the next day, his father kept him out the rest of the week. Over the weekend, Rafe had kept up with his school work by checking the school's secure website. He hoped he wasn't too far behind. He tried focusing on that, rather than what he might face. So he went up the steps quickly and then became a robot.

Rafe zipped down the hallway, his eyes on the floor tiles. He didn't want to meet anyone's eyes.

Rafe made it to his locker without meeting anybody he knew. It was early enough that most of the students hadn't come in, and snow, even light snow, could hold up traffic. There was a note in his locker, apparently shoved through one of the grates. It was a folded piece of blue graph paper. Just holding it, Rafe knew it was nothing good. It burned with dark energy. He sighed, placed the note in his algebra text book, and went on to home room.

As he expected, the class was half empty. Theo looked up from his cell phone; Rafe could tell from the spooked look Theo gave him that Theo had seen whatever nasty things were flying around the Internet about him. Rafe took his seat next to Theo and ignored him.

❖

He and his father had visited Ursele on Saturday. They brought a slice of fruit-topped cheesecake from her favorite bakery and watched her eat it in the patient's lounge. She'd looked a little out of it—she'd been adjusting the medicine, which apparently took several weeks to be fully effective. The lounge's cinderblock walls were covered with motivational posters, and a TV blared music videos.

❖

Rafe opened his algebra book and took out the note.

❖

After she'd finished the cheesecake, Rafe's mother said that she would like to speak to Rafe alone. His father moved over to the other side of the room, where a stack of magazines beckoned.

❖

Rafe unfolded the note, and saw the sloppy, lopsided handwriting on it. It had a squashed feel. He kind of recognized it.

❖

Rafe's mother said, once his father was out of earshot, "Your father... Sam... told me what happened at school. About the fight. I'm sorry that I haven't been there for you. I don't know what I could've done, really. I just want you to stay strong. I know you can. Forget those glass things. *You* are my angel, Rafael."

❖

The note read:

Rafe:

Don't know what happened in the locker room with your boy Toby. Don't want to know. I think he's a fag anyway. Are you one too? Don't want to know. No offense, but can't be seen hanging around no faggots. No homo here, ha ha. Don't take it personal.

Sideshow

So. Tomás was an asshole. And a coward. And not his friend. Rafe crumpled the note up and crushed it until it was small, as small as it could be.

He looked up and saw Theo and Oglivy looking at him. *Screw them*, he thought. *Let them look*. Then he remembered Q's story. And he knew how Q had felt. How easy it would be to bring a knife or a gun to school and end the torment right then and there. Just as his mother had shattered the angels, he saw himself doing the same with these evil kids. These orcs. Let them piss him off. He'd show them-

More kids came shuffling in, their shoes and hair jeweled with melting snowflakes. The flakes sparkled like glass.

This is gonna be too much. I should leave.

O'Connell walked into the classroom and seemed to do a double-take when he saw Rafe. He smiled at Rafe, then called the class to order and started the prayer. Afterward, O'Connell approached Rafe.

"Rafael," he said, in front of the class, who all pretended not to notice—shuffling papers, conversations hushed—"don't hesitate to come to me, if you want to talk." O'Connell put his hand on Rafe's shoulder and gave it a slight squeeze.

And Rafe knew, just *knew*, that O'Connell was aware of the rumors about the shower, about Toby. He knew he could go to O'Connell and get comfort, if he wanted. They could talk about geeky things, like comic books and fantasy novels and gaming. Rafe would be under O'Connell's wing. He would be safe in that red sanctuary, in that tiny office. The office where the drawing of a nude brown boy hid beneath other drawings of saints and papers about religion. *What else did that office hide?* The Luminous Lady wouldn't tell.

Rafe remembered her, a few days ago, telling him to leave the office after he'd seen that drawing.

Rafe shrugged O'Connell's hand off him. He gave a noncommittal nod and pretended to be interested in something else. He dug around in his book bag, until he pulled up his cell phone. He flipped it open and waited until O'Connell had left his side.

Rafe saw that he had a text on his phone's screen. He sighed—probably one of the orcs had found his phone number. He clicked on the icon and opened the text.

"Hope yr doing OK. Memba: Yr betta than them. F em all! --Q :-)"

Rafe smiled.

The rest of the morning, other students kept away from Rafe. Freeman and Mercanti assiduously avoided eye contact during their shared classes, but he'd catch them and sometimes others glancing at him. Rafe only heard snickering once, during gym class. Toby was there, of course, but he didn't look at Rafe, and Loomis made sure that they were separated. During the shower, Rafe slipped in and out as quickly as he could. He overheard boys one row over talking about how icky faggots were. Toby said, loudly, how he'd personally pound the living shit out of any *butt pirate* who made a pass at him.

Rafe dressed quickly and retrieved his cell phone.

He texted Q, "They're starting again."

Not a minute later, Q texted back: "It's not about u. He's f'd up. Ignore him."

Rafe texted back a smiley face.

"Talking to your boyfriend, *Gayfe*?" Toby brushed by Rafe.

"Why are you asking? Want one of your own?" Rafe left the locker room. He heard laughter, but he was unsure whether or not they were laughing at him or at Toby. He realized that he didn't care.

Lunch was a rubbery chicken cutlet in a perfect circle with pale golden breading that wasn't crisp enough, a succotash dish with wan corn and lima beans, nuclearyellow macaroni and cheese, and a chocolate pudding that oozed water. It would probably be Rafe's only substantial meal of the day. His father wouldn't be back home until after nine o'clock. It was nice having his father around, in a way. But Rafe still missed his mother. Soon she would be released from the hospital. *What would she be like then?* Rafe heard that the psych meds sometimes turned folks into emotional zombies—that wasn't any better than Ursele being super-religious.

As he walked down the cafeteria aisle, he saw Sideshow sitting with Rahul. He moved away from them and opted to sit at the end of a table full of other loners, mostly kids doing their homework. Rafe opened up a book—he was still reading *A Game of Thrones*—and read while he devoured his lunch, trying hard not pay attention to the flavors.

So. This how it's gonna be for the rest of my time at Our Shady Lady.

He would be alone. Maybe that wasn't so bad—he'd get a lot of reading done.

"Hey."

Rafe looked up from his book. Rahul sat down across from him.

"Hey," Rafe said and put the book away.

"Mind if I sit here?"

"Don't see why not. You know that Sideshow hates me."

Rahul rolled his eyes. "I know. He's kind of an asshole."

Rafe laughed, and it felt good. It was the kind of laugh that comes from the soul and permeates every molecule.

Maybe he wouldn't be alone after all.

FINDING THE MASK

There is a signal. It's not quite a song or even a sound, but it has a sonic resonance, a kind of sub-vibration. Rafe finds himself in his mother's closet, moving aside the racks of empty dresses, pushing aside storage containers full of accessories. He unearths the mask, which has been hidden behind a thick shawl. Uncovered, the Dan mask stares at him, with eye slits and cowrie shells intact.

The mask's lips are parted. Were they that way before? Rafe can't remember—it's been months since his mother hid it away because of its "dark energy." But, in spite of disagreeing with his mother's actions, Rafe understands why she was scared of the mask. It's because the mask does have a weird, thrumming power emanating from it.

Rafe extracts the mask from the back of the closet, and takes it back to his room. What is his mother going to do about it? She's supposed to get better—any day now, the drugs will kick in and quell her manias. There's good reason to believe that she won't freak out.

He puts the mask back in its spot in his bedroom, hanging it on the lonely nail that sticks out of the wall above his bed. Back home.

Once the mask is there, everything just feels right. The air is sweeter, the light less harsh.

Rafe smiles, feeling more like himself than he has in months. He tries to figure what, exactly, the feeling is.

Basking in the warm, "dark" energy of the face on wall, Rafe identifies the unnamed emotion.

He no longer feels alone.

About the Author

Craig Laurance Gidney writes both young adult and genre fiction. Recipient of the 1996 Susan C. Petrey Scholarship to the Clarion West writer's workshop, Gidney has published works in the fantasy/science fiction, gay, and young adult categories.

These works include "A Bird of Ice" (from the Lethe Press anthology *So Fey: Queer Fairy Fiction*), which was on the short list for the 2008 Gaylactic Spectrum Award; "The Safety of Thorns," which received special notice by editor Ellen Datlow in her 2006 *Year's Best Fantasy Horror* summary; "Mauve's Quilt" (from the young adult fantasy anthology *Magic in the Mirrorstone*, published by Wizards of the Coast); and "Circus Boy Without a Safety Net," included in the anthology *From Where We Sit: Black Writers Write Black Youth* (Tiny Satchel Press). Gidney's first collection of short stories, *Sea, Swallow Me and Other Stories* (Lethe Press), was nominated for the 2009 Lambda Literary Award in the science fiction/fantasy/horror category. *Bereft* is his first novel. Gidney is an editor and lives in Washington, D.C.

Acknowledgments

Thanks to Victoria A. Brownworth and Tiny Satchel Press for giving me the opportunity to bring *Bereft* to a wider audience.